SWAN DIVE

SWAN DIVE

◆ ◆ ◆

MICHAEL BURKE

Pleasure Boat Studio: A Literary Press
New York
2009

Swan Dive
by Michael Burke

ISBN 978-1-929355-50-1
Library of Congress Control Number: 2008941343

Design by Susan Ramundo
Cover by Laura Tolkow
Cover painting by Gunilla Feigenbaum

Caravel Books is a mystery imprint of Pleasure Boat Studio: A Literary Press. Pleasure Boat Studio is a proud subscriber to the Green Press Initiative. This program encourages the use of 100% post-consumer recycled paper with environmentally friendly inks for all printing projects in an effort to reduce the book industry's economic and social impact. With the cooperation of our printing company, we are pleased to offer this book as a Green Press book.

Pleasure Boat Studio books are available through the following:
SPD (Small Press Distribution) Tel. 800-869-7553, Fax 510-524-0852
Partners/West Tel. 425-227-8486, Fax 425-204-2448
Baker & Taylor Tel. 800-775-1100, Fax 800-775-7480
Ingram Tel. 615-793-5000, Fax 615-287-5429
Amazon.com and **bn.com**

and through
PLEASURE BOAT STUDIO: A LITERARY PRESS
www.pleasureboatstudio.com
201 West 89th Street
New York, NY 10024

Contact **Jack Estes**
Fax: 888-810-5308
Email: *pleasboat@nyc.rr.com*

"For even daughters of the swan can share
Something of every paddler's heritage . . ."

"Among School Children"
W. B. Yeats

PROLOGUE

Every year the earth travels around the sun. During the summer months, rays of sunlight strike the earth directly—it is hot. As the earth proceeds on an elliptical path, she flies nearer to the sun, but as she tilts on her axis the warming rays become slanted, spreading more thinly over the land. Summer heat becomes fall cool. Ducks, geese and herons begin to fly south. From Canada, they fly along the eastern coast of New England, passing over rocky beaches and cliffs that drop steeply into the Atlantic. They fly over forests where leaves are turning red and orange, over pine groves and maples, maples by the thousands pushing out the birches, the oaks, and the sycamores. The migrating birds are pushed towards the earth by threatening storm clouds. They sail over meadows, farms, homes and mansions cut into the green. As night falls, patterns of light appear beneath, where one castle glows, where figures mill about on the terrace, where limousines are parked in solemn rows, where the dark of the forest fights with the light streaming from the celebration inside. A figure stands outside the sphere of light, behind a tall hedge, hesitating, unsure of his direction. He turns, stops. Spasms shake his body. He drops to his knees and calls to the sky for help. He falls to the ground, twisting and writhing. His cries fall on deaf ears as the party continues inside. His feet kick, digging up clumps of grass, forming a circle of agony cut into the lawn. Slowly, he stops moving, and lies alone, silent, on the grass, by the hedge, in the dark, out of sight.

1

SHE FLOATED TOWARD ME, a yellow sash of gossamer gold fluttering about her waist. I knew what she wanted and how to supply it. I'd been watching her, the seductive move, the glance in my direction, the knowing look . . .

"What are ya staring at, mister?" woke me from my daydream.

"Your apron," I mumbled, "trying to read it."

"Says 'Ralph's Pizza,' and on the back side, 'All You Can Eat.' Now finish that crust and get going. We're supposed to be closed for ten minutes already."

"S'pose I finish my beer first."

"Look, big guy. I'm turning off the lights. You can either head home or we can go in the back and you can screw me on the salad bar."

❖   ❖   ❖

I turned on to Machinist's Drive, headed for my apartment in the Gold Hill Arms, a name someone had thought up in better days. Dung Hill Arms was a better name for it. The Arms was once a rooming house, a six-story brick building that sat uncomfortably amid the abandoned factories. Back when the work was good, plentiful, and needed, the factories hummed twenty-four hours a day, and the Arms had beds for the workers who came and went with the seasons. Now only a few of the industries were hanging on. I passed Iron, Inc., the rambling metal works that survived by supplying reinforcing rods for construction that took place in distant cities. It was protected by a fifteen-foot-high rusted iron fence, and the rods were stacked in dangerously unstable piles. Pharm-a-Lot was next, a pharmaceutical plant that was doing quite well keeping the drug culture supplied. I buy sleeping pills from their factory store to use when the vodka doesn't work. I drove by two abandoned hulks, concrete shells with empty black holes where glass used to keep out the cold. Factories that produced I don't know what, but whatever it was it is now made overseas for ten cents an hour. Next, and closest to the Arms, an unnamed asphalt plant puffed and fumed. It survives because our highways have an infinite number of potholes to be filled. It was Monday night and the air was carrying a damp fall chill that held the noxious fumes close to the ground.

Sunday nights were easier. They held out a promise for the week ahead that kept dreams alive. By Monday, however, I had to accept the truth that nothing was about to change. I pulled the fifteen-year-old Honda Accord around to the side of the Arms and parked by the van with the two flat tires that hadn't moved from that spot for as long as I could remember.

There was a nip in the air, a premonition of the cold months to come. Winter constellations were beginning to take their place in the sky. The stars in Orion's belt were bright enough to fight for attention with the crescent moon, which hung low in the east and cast a colorless light to frame the dark shadows on the pavement. The earth was three weeks away from featuring a full harvest moon and still waiting for the first frost of the season. Leaves were abandoning the trees and rustling about the street, their bright daylight colors, orange and red in the sun, were lost in the black and white of night vision. Night time: I read about a man who, because of a conk on the head, became totally color-blind. He couldn't make love to his wife because her skin color reminded him of a rat. He ended up living after the sun set— one doesn't see much color at night. It's a world of grays and misfits. Monday night, and I was looking forward to a week of empty days. I nodded to the night watchman.

"Good evening Mister Heron," he said politely. Javier was the only guy who worked here who knew my name, perhaps because I seldom saw the daytime crew. "A message for you, sir."

"Yes, what?"

"A Mr. Fuller came by and left this note. He said if you got in before midnight to give him a call."

"Thanks, pal, I'll call him in the morning." Maybe the curse of the Mondays had been broken. The week threatened to put me to work, a job, a purpose, and some money to be made. I climbed the back stairs to 3C, my two-and-a-half-room palace, with river view (if you leaned out the window) and AC (when working). It had given me a home for longer than I cared to remember.

2

THE OFFICE OF FULLER Investments was downtown, a couple of blocks away from the town square on the fourth floor of a no-nonsense professional building filled with dentists, doctors, and travel agents who ran a thriving business helping people escape from Dullsville. Nothing fancy. The building was modern drab—the lobby reminded me of a crypt where some second-rate politician was interred. The paper taped to the elevator door announcing 'out of service' was yellowing from age. I climbed the three flights to Fuller's Office. I wasn't buzzed in until I gave my name, rank, and serial number. The small reception area was governed by a Ms. Marie Henry, according to the sign plate by her in-box. Ms. Henry had dark black hair, black eyes, and a complexion that made me doubt the name Henry. She focused on me as though I was an imposter and she could see clear through my disguise.

"You don't look like you're here for financial advice. Just what is your business?" Ms. Henry asked suspiciously.

"Whatever Fuller told you is what I am. How about you tell him I'm here."

Ms. Henry obliged and buzzed her boss on the intercom. There was an indistinct mumble on the other end that prompted Ms. Henry to say, "Mr. Fuller is expecting you. Come this way."

We passed a side office where I could see the backs of a couple of assistants poring over their computer screens. A young woman caught my eye, not an unusual occurrence, I admit, but she seemed to be too pretty to be studying a computer screen. My image of computers involved teenaged nerds with overdeveloped thumbs blowing away strange techno-generated beasts for hours at a time. I probably was jealous, but I was proud of my newly learned skills. I could now use Wikipedia, type, print out stuff, and play Minesweeper at the intermediate level. This lady didn't fit the mold. Glasses that turned up at the edges, straight brown hair cut neatly parallel with the earth's surface, and tight sheer stockings that reflected the fluorescent light in constantly shifting patterns. They would no doubt make a lovely sound when rubbed together. A legal assistant no doubt, compliments of one of the Seven Sisters. She glanced over at me with a 'if you could quit staring it would be nice' look. I smiled and followed Ms. Henry through the frosted glass door to Mr. Fuller's inner sanctum.

George Fuller sat behind a large polished wooden desk that appeared to be handed down from the founding fathers. On the wall behind him, in place of the usual array of diplomas, citations, and awards, hung a large gold-framed map of the U.S. as it appeared in the 19th Century. The side walls displayed historic black-and-white photographs of city scenes. One featured the old benches in our town square. An old-fashioned ink well, a quill pen, and a square bronze paperweight sat on the otherwise empty desk. The only thing in the room that was the least bit disheveled was Fuller himself. He was a handsome man, with a thin nose and engaging eyes, but the striped tie was a bit out of kilter and he was missing a button on his suit coat. Probably a ladykiller in his youth, now he had just enough gray in his hair to suggest that some respect would be appreciated.

"You're a private eye," Mr. Fuller muttered more to himself than to me.

"I like Expert in Exotic Research, myself."

"Yes, yes, well I've never hired one of your type before. Yes, where do we start?"

I answered with film noir expertise. "I've heard all the questions so let me help you out: $500 a day, expenses, guarantee a week, and we can talk it over after that. You tell me what you want to know, I tell you what I find out, and the rest is up to you. I don't ask questions, and you don't ask me how I get information. You probably wouldn't want to know anyway."

"That, ah, sounds a bit harsh, you know."

"It's private eye lingo—I can make it gentler. What is it that's troubling you? I'll try to help."

"Oh yes, I, ah, need to know about someone. I mean does she, this person exist, and, ah, who is she?" Mr. Fuller was not at ease with the private eye thing, and I suspected his discomfort fed the "ah, yes" stutter.

I had checked out the Fuller Investment web site before I came by. It was clean and straight-forward and not filled with fancy effects. I didn't have much experience in the financial world, but I couldn't imagine how the slogan "The Fuller the Better" helped attract clients. That, combined with

the disheveled look and the 'ahs' and 'yesses' that were sprinkled about made me wonder about the whole operation. In
order to help this conversation along and get Fuller to quit
over-thinking the deal, I said, "All right, just make it simple.
Who, what, where, when—no need for why."

"Yes. My boy Castor, you see, he's married. Well, not
quite married, but they're engaged. To a nice girl, yes, very
nice. In fact she works here. Legal assistant, very bright."

I guessed that I'd been staring at her legs a moment ago.
"Good family, respectable," I suggested. "All that, and probably rich too, right?"

"Yes, she's very, ah, very proper, but . . ."

"But?"

"I think her husband, ah, fiancé, my son, is seeing someone on the side, behind her back. That's not good. I'd like to
know more about it."

"You haven't spoken with him?"

"Well, ah, yes, sort of. I mean we don't share everything.
I asked him if everything was fine and he got a bit, ah, de-
fensive. I'm afraid we tend to talk in circles."

"His mother, what does she know?" I asked.

"She's not around," Fuller said abruptly. "So if you discover anything just keep it quiet, yes? And report to me."

"It shouldn't be too hard to track something down—a
couple of names and addresses, maybe a photo if you have
one. I should be able to find the lady without too much trouble. A simple tail should turn up something pretty quickly.
People don't tend to be too smart about covering up these
things." I could see that Mr. Fuller did not want to tell me

what he expected to do with the information. He probably hadn't figured that out himself.

He gave me the full names: his son, Castor Fuller, and Castor's live-in lover, Beverly Whitney. The photograph of Castor looked like a head shot for a modeling agency. There was something familiar about her last name, but then Whitney had money written all over it. I couldn't pin down what Fuller was really after; maybe he wanted to get his hands on some of the cash.

I recognized their address—it was one of a cluster of small homes on Loudon Street that struggled to survive behind the new Main Street Mall. The Mall was on Main Street, but about a half mile away from the city center. By language alone it was declaring itself the new center of town.

I picked up the photos, wrote down the names and, resisting the urge to stuff it all into my coat pocket, slid them into the folder that Fuller handed me. I could ditch the folder later. Mr. George Fuller was not comfortable with the transaction and obviously wanted the meeting to end. I said I'd let him know in a day or two if I found Castor's sleepover partner, bade him good-day, and opened the office door. It clanged against the top drawer of a filing cabinet that Marie Henry was thumbing through. She snatched out a paper, pushed the drawer shut, and, with a brief apology, returned to her desk. Seems Ms. Henry decided to do her filing in the closest drawer she could find to Fuller's office door. Well, I had no exclusive rights to the spying business. On the way back to the car I kicked around the idea that we are all spies and deep down inside we all want to be caught.

3

MY NEXT STOP WAS the police precinct. Experience told me to check out what the professionals already knew before wasting time trying to uncover everything myself. I knew the place inside and out, had spent some years on the law enforcement payroll. Chief Inspector JJ Cakes and I went back a long way, and I always looked for an excuse to see Kathy. Kathy was there at the desk, more beautiful than I had remembered. She looked up at me with wide misleadingly innocent eyes from under a fountain of soft brown hair, hair that would drop over her eye on cue whenever I stared too hard. She was wearing a suit with a skirt just a bit too short to co-exist with her rank, Inspector McGregor. We had tried to get together a few times but something, probably me, always messed it up. Nothing seemed to worry her, and that generally made me grouchy. I thought she never cared too much if I was there or not, but there were still sparks and she loved to remind me of what I was missing.

"Well hi there, sweety," she cooed. "You've no doubt come to see me." Kathy was JJ's right-hand man, a no-nonsense researcher who could dig up dirt on the Pope's sex life if it would solve a case. In another line of work she would be sitting in JJ's chair, but this was the police department and even in these enlightened times I've never met a cop who could tolerate taking orders from a lady.

I pretended to be above it all. "JJ, is he back there?"

"Give him a minute, Corbutt's in there. What's new, Blue? When are we going to the movies?"

"Kathy, you're talking to a guy who sees the world as though he's watching a movie."

"I like the way you look at things, all upside down and backwards, but I agree, sometimes you're hopeless."

Officer Corbutt came out of JJ's office. He was tall and wide and the muscles in his arms tested the strength of the policeman's blue fabric. Eggs and steroids for breakfast. He gave Kathy a warm smile and ignored me on the way through. I gave him the mental finger.

"You can go in now." Kathy turned to buzz her boss, leading the turn with one leg, displaying a tunnel of promise between her thighs.

"No need to buzz—I'll show myself in." I tried to look straight ahead as I pushed into the office. JJ was there, short and solid. He had shaved his head a few years back to avoid dealing with a growing bald spot. Now it clearly reflected the light of an overhead fluorescent fixture. He looked like a pushover, but the end of a jagged scar that peeked over his collar testified to a man toughened by years on the force. He was half hidden by the pile on the long table that masqueraded as his desk, where no surface was left uncluttered. Precinct reports were covered by last week's newspapers, and mug shots of murderers were mixed with pictures of Cindy and the kids.

"Well if it isn't Blue," he said brightly. The guys at the precinct liked to call me Blue. "Hey how are you, Blue? How's life? How are they hanging? What's new? What do you want to know?"

"You're looking good JJ. The promotion suits you."

"Specially the money," he agreed.

"Fuller, George Fuller. Heads up an investment outfit, has an assistant Beverly Whitney. She and his son are planning on getting hitched. Do you know the names?"

"I've met Fuller. In fact, that's why you're on the case. He called. Wanted some work done but he was very vague. I think he was trying to find out if it was legal to hire a private eye. I gave him your name."

"Thanks JJ. I'll try to keep it above board."

"Don't know very much about his operation. It's pretty small time. But I wonder if the Whitney you're talking about is the daughter of Douglas Whitney, of Whitney and Whitney and, nope, no sons. She's an only child. Whitney wanted a son of course, but got Beverly. Bright girl, a lawyer. So she's engaged to Fuller's kid. Seems odd she'd be working for a competitor of her Daddy. Anyway, what's the problem? What's he got you doing?"

"It's the usual: sneaking around, spying on people's sex lives. Can't tell you much more right now because that's what I'm getting paid to find out, and with my income I'd better get some results."

"Too bad you left us Blue—at least there's steady pay here." JJ was well aware of my need for some dollars.

"I do miss it sometimes," I agreed. "Punching in at eight-thirty every morning, making small talk over the water cooler, acting busy, counting the hours left in the day, and sleeping in the toilet stall. Now when the clock shows eight o'clock, I roll over and go back to sleep. What more could I ask for?"

"Can't imagine," JJ joked. "Sounds like you have it all, except for a life, of course, but that can be highly over-rated. By the way, I may need some help next week. There's a guy who needs some police presence, and I would like to take along an undercover, someone who is not identified with us but knows the cop stuff. They won't think you're a flatfoot—you're too good looking to be on the force. Are you up for a bit of freelance, if it comes through?"

"Any time." I saluted and headed for the door. "Thanks, JJ. I'll let you know if I find out anything."

"I trust you mean that as 'I'll let you know if I need anything.'" Then JJ added, "Good luck, Blue, and by the way, you should check out the financial stuff with 'Doctor Dollar.' He'll know for sure."

On the way out I tried to walk by Kathy without registering the pink triangle that winked at me from under her skirt.

"See you Kathy. Maybe we should have a drink someday."

"Why should I want to do that?" came the curt response.

"Next week, how about?"

"Next week. Oh sure." She sighed. "Next week."

4

I LEFT THE POLICE headquarters and was walking by the park before an unfamiliar spark of good sense caught up with me. I turned and headed back inside. Muscles Corbutt, sitting at the front desk, gave me a 'you again' look. A line-up of robbers and rapists accompanied by their police escorts was waiting for the elevator, so I took the back stairs to Kathy's office.

"Whatcha doin'? How about a beer?" I said as casually as I could, considering I was wheezing from taking three flights, two stairs at a time.

Kathy looked up, obviously amused. "Ten minutes, meet you out front."

I gave Corbutt a wave and a smile as I passed back through the lobby. It didn't seem to cheer him up.

Kathy and I walked the two blocks to Leroy's Bar, the bar that catered to the three faces of the court: the lawyers, the cops, and the crooks. You could easily walk by Leroy's and never notice it. A simple door beside the hardware store had an opaque glass pane that said LEROY'S in block letters. Not even LEROY'S BAR. It could be two in the afternoon on a bright sunny day, but in Leroy's a couple could feel they were meeting in the dark of night. Sharing beers with Kathy had the feel of an illicit affair, but to me any contact with Kathy felt like an illicit affair.

"Haven't seen you guys for a while," Leroy greeted us from behind the bar. He was surprisingly disarming for a guy who looked like a hit man for the Mafia. "Same old? Two drafts?"

"You have a good memory," Kathy said.

The place was nearly empty. Behind the bar were four impressive rows of bottles, liquors I had never heard of and looked forward to trying out. To the sides hung photographs of young Leroy standing with movie stars, sports heroes, and politicians. A loner sat on a stool, his elbows welded to the bar, and a couple sitting at a corner table talked in guilty whispers. Kathy and I decided on a spot on the other side of the room.

"So," Kathy started, "what's up?" Kathy looked me directly in the eye, forming a sight line so intense that Phillipe Petit could have walked between us.

"Just thought I'd tell you I got a job," I boasted. "I'm joining the ranks of the gainfully employed."

Kathy frowned. "Blue, your idea of gainfully employed is what, a spy job that's good for a week or two?"

"What would the world do without a good spy? There's plenty of doers—they're a dime a dozen. But a good observer, that's special."

"I admit, you do have talent as a looker, both giving and receiving." She brushed a rebellious lock of hair from her forehead.

"Was that a compliment?"

"You could get yourself a job at Chippendales. Make a killing on tips stuffed into your jock."

"Can't dance."

"You can say that again. So, tell me, what's the case? Who hired you?"

"This guy called police headquarters. JJ psyched out that he was looking for a private eye, and sent him to me."

"Good for JJ. Anybody I'd know?" Kathy asked.

"It's Fuller Investments. Actually I'm not supposed to give out details."

"Maybe I can help." Kathy surprised me. "I know a bit about Fuller's son, Castor."

"Really?"

"He is an aspiring actor. He's good at it, and handsome too. But he doesn't make any money to speak of."

"How do you know him?"

"I saw him down at the public theatre. A sexy part, and he was good. I did a teenage stage-door thing afterwards and caught his eye. We got along. One thing led to another—you know how it is."

"I understand that jaws drop when his pants drop," I said, feeling clever.

"Oh yes, there is that," Kathy answered off-handedly. Then, catching herself, "How did you know about it?"

"It was supposed to be a joke; now I wish I hadn't heard the punch line."

"Problem was, he always had some excuse and left me with the tab. Then Ms. Whitney and her dollars came along, and I was history."

"Did you meet his dad?"

"Yes, briefly. He is a strange dude. From the Midwest I think, and a bit out of his element. Between the two of them there's a perpetual lack of cash."

"Was the Whitney girl working for him?"

"Girl? C'mon, she's pushing thirty. No, she started after they got engaged. She was working in her father's office, and I have a feeling that she moved over to Fuller to save her sanity. She's bright and capable, but never got along very well with her dad."

Leroy came by with two more pint glasses. "On the house," he said, setting them down. I figured he was trying to get our business back.

"So you're on your own now?" I asked.

Kathy looked over her glass, "There's always Corbutt."

"That guy's a loser," I grumbled. "How come you always end up with would-be actors or deadbeats? We should get back together. I meet all the criteria."

Kathy laughed, "Anytime, Blue."

"Sounds good, but Kathy you should never trust me. Find yourself a real guy, someone whose outside is the same as their inside. Someone whose mind isn't controlled by aliens from outer space, who knows the difference between love and the first black-and-white porn photos he saw in ninth grade."

"I know," Kathy sighed. "You do see the world from a strange angle. Unfortunately I rather like that. It's a bit of the artist in you."

"I always did like the Fauvists. Make up your own colors."

Leroy's was beginning to fill as lawyers who left their desks early were filing through the door. The lawyers could leave their jobs whenever they wanted; the clerks had to punch the clock, so they wouldn't be coming in 'til after the five o-clock hour. Their clients tended to come in after midnight. We got up from the table, nodded to Leroy, and stepped out on the street. The sun was still bright enough to have a sobering effect, which I needed for the drive home.

"See you, Kathy. Thanks for the input."

"See you," she said.

We walked off in opposite directions.

5

CASTOR AND BEVERLY DIDN'T live far from the center and there was still time left in the day to begin checking them out, but the sun was thinking about dropping behind the mountains to the west, and I was thinking of sitting in my favorite, well, my only, armchair with a martini and the yet-untouched morning paper. There'd be time enough tomorrow. I started the drive home. There wasn't any pattern to the layout of this town—sitting on the outskirts of Boston had left it with an identity crisis. Apartment blocks appeared next to ranch-style homes, and convenience stores and fast-food drive-ins were sprinkled about, as though dropped from a low-flying plane. One thing I was sure of, though, and that was that the traffic lights had been meticulously programmed to turn red when they spotted the approach of my Honda. Finally I turned onto Machinist's Drive, back into the landscape of concrete shells, rusting fuel tanks, and unwanted machines parked randomly on buckling asphalt. Scattered in between were lonely brick apartment buildings that served as homes for people who couldn't afford a richer rent, who were running from something, or who wanted to live on the outside and look in. I tried out the good life, but chose this, living with the observers of the world. Preachers say you get what you deserve, so a two-and-a-half-room flat in the factory district was fair. And I have a balcony, and a western view over the railyards to the river, glorious sunsets, and all the time I need. I'm okay with this. I suppose I'm just too contrary to be satisfied with green grass and a leaf blower. I was raised with the belief that if you were accepted, praised, and rewarded, you were probably selling out. It's the role of the artist, except I'm not an artist. Maybe that's the flaw. Who would have thought that sleeping through four years of art history and mythology would land me a job in the police department working on an art forgery case. JJ kept me on, but I was more interested in the forgeries than the real thing. Always thought I was a fake, but aren't we all? We invent ourselves and defy the world to discover the ruse.

Near the historic Dung Hill Arms, I passed a car parked by the side of the road. Normally this wouldn't be unusual— our street was dark and unused enough to offer parking areas for couples who wanted a quiet spot to discuss which of Shakespeare's plays was their favorite, but this car was big, black, and brand new, and definitely out of place. I drove into my usual parking spot next to the rusty van and turned off the lights. I'd read enough detective stories to know what would happen next. Instead of walking to the front door, I stopped and waited around the corner, close enough to the edge of the building to allow me to keep an eye on the car. Just as scripted, the limo started to move slowly down the street in my direction. It fit the bill, polished and shined until the black skin hurt, obviously chauffeured, windows dark enough to set my imagination into high gear. When it pulls up next to me, I thought, and the window rolls part way down, and the barrel of a 45 pokes out, I'll drop behind the van and fire. No use shooting at the windows—they will be bullet proof. Shooting out the tires might stop a getaway, but that wouldn't make me any safer. Had to aim for the gas tank, probably low under the middle of the car, closer to the rear wheel. Three or so well-placed shots low in front of the back wheel . . . .

The limo stopped, the driver's side door opened, and a man in a chauffeur's uniform stepped out. He was about six-six, 250 pounds cap and all, with lots of brass buttons.

"Johnny Heron?" was all he said.

"That's me."

He walked around to my side of the car. "My boss wants to talk to you." It wasn't a question.

"So where do I find this guy who's so interested in me?" I tried to make myself as tall as I could but my six-foot-two still gave away a couple of inches.

"Right here," he said, opening the back door. "Get in."

I hadn't been inside one of these boats since my senior prom. The figure inside gestured me in and I obliged. As soon as Brass Buttons closed the car door behind me, I began to regret the decision. The inside of the limo was like a small sitting room, with a bar, fridge, TV, and bullet-proof tinted windows. The figure sitting opposite me was wearing a black suit, with black shoes and black socks. He had a large head with hair too black for his age, unblinking dead eyes, and a fraternity tie with a gold icon that suggested he was a member of Skull and Bones. The rest of him was small but the confines made him grow in stature.

"We should talk," was his greeting.

The tone of the word 'talk' suggested that only one of us was going to be doing the talking, but it didn't look like anybody was going to get shot, at least not right away. I answered as nicely as possible, "Nice to meet you, Mr. ah . . . ."

"Whitney, Douglas Whitney. We haven't met." He pulled aside a glass panel that separated him from the gorilla, who had returned to the front seat and ordered, "Find a place to park where we won't be too conspicuous."

"There's a graveyard at the end of the street," I volunteered. "This car will fit right in." Did I just suggest that a nasty-looking black limo with a thug in front and a boss man in back drive me to a cemetery? I should get a day job before it's too late.

"A drink?" he offered.

"Not unless I can have one to go."

He ignored me. Took a brandy snifter from the bar and poured himself a stiff drink on the rocks. The diamond on his finger rivaled the ice cube for size.

"Now," Whitney began, "I understand that George has hired you for some detective work."

"George?" How does he know that already I wondered. I was in Fuller's office only this morning.

"Don't play dumb with me, Johnny." He liked the familiar. "George Fuller. So what's the job?" Mr. Whitney apparently expected his questions to be answered.

"Look, Mr. Big Car"—I thought that was a good retort—"maybe you should quit asking me questions that you're not going to get answers to, and fill me in a bit, or we're getting nowhere." Except we'd already gotten as far as the cemetery.

He pulled back a bit, trying to appear a bit less threatening. "You've got me wrong, Johnny. There's nothing illegal here, I'm Douglas Whitney. You may have heard of Whitney and Whitney, Investments. Well, that's me. I've been working with Fuller for a while now. In fact we're planning to merge. Bigger companies have an advantage these days, and we hope to put together a strong operation." Whitney was talking like a thug one minute, and an ivy-league-business-suiter the next. From "O Sole Mio" to "The Whiffenpoof Song" without changing the key.

"But first you'll need some official approval," I tossed out, hoping to show that I knew what he was talking about.

"Exactly, but if you get in there, and start digging up dirt, or a supposed scandal, or whatever it is that you guys get paid for, it gets in the way. I don't want that to happen." The friendly tone didn't last long and the back seat was beginning to feel like the inside of locked bank vault.

"Mr. Whitney. I've got nothing against you, but I'm not working for you. I'm, shall we say, a bit of a free spirit as far as you're concerned."

"Well, maybe you'd like to work for me."

"I don't like to turn down jobs, but it sounds like there could be a conflict of interest here."

"You private eyes are always looking for evil motives. This is straight up. I want this merger, Fuller wants the merger. It's good for the young couple, Beverly and Castor; they get the benefits of being part of a good solid business. Everybody wins."

"Everybody?" I asked.

"Yes, Johnny, even you." He reached into an inside coat pocket. I expected a gun to appear, but he pulled out a block of bills. It was one of those packets that you only see in the movies, nicely stacked and bound together with a paper strip. I could see Mr. Franklin's hundred dollar image and suppressed an urge to reach out and riffle through the pack as though taking count. In films, bundles of cash like this are usually found in a black briefcase, and are neatly packed in rows that perfectly fill the case, and the bad guys wave guns around and empty the cash into burlap bags and drive off, and there's a car chase, and a gun fight, and the sacks would be all shot up and bills would be blowing all over the wharf, and then she drops in from above, spinning and raising one long leg high enough to kick away the machine gun, wearing . . . .

"Everybody wins. Even you," Whitney repeated, pushing the bundle toward me.

"I've never played in any games where everybody wins, and I don't think this is a good time to start," I said. "Sorry, I can't be of service." I opened the door. "I'll walk back. A stroll through the cemetery and a drink might cheer me up."

"Best be careful what you're drinking, Mr. Heron. Never know what's in it," Whitney growled.

I didn't hear what else Whitney said before I closed the car door, and I didn't want to hear what he said. The limo pulled away. I looked at the graves.

6

WEDNESDAY MORNING AND THE blue Honda was reluctant to start before the sun had warmed her fifteen-year-old frame. At first she refused to acknowledge the starter motor at all, then with some kicks and sputters and a cloud of black smoke in the rear-view mirror, she grudgingly woke up, and we backed out onto the roadway. I needed to get an early start to make sure I was watching Castor's front door before anyone left for work. A half hour later I drove through the back of the Main Street Mall parking lot and turned on to Loudon Street. I found a spot and the end of the street, shaded by a grand sycamore tree that was slowly shaking off its summer leaves. Stakeouts are probably the most boring occupation ever schemed up. Sit in a car, park close enough to watch a doorway, far enough away not to look suspicious. If the car was the right color, a pastel, and you were the right color, white, and there were no peace stickers on the bumper, you'd probably be left alone. "Honk For Jesus" stickers were okay. Older people tended not to stare, but kids on bicycles, or even worse, tricycles, were the scourges of a stakeout. They'd come up to the car and press their noses against the window. This street was quiet, however, and I could relax with a newspaper propped against the steering wheel and a cup of lukewarm coffee. On a good day I'd have a buttered bagel. I've found that I am particularly well suited for this kind of work, as I had refined daydreaming into an art form. And thinking of Kathy—my subscription to *The Weekly Wanker*—provided plenty of material for lively scripts to play out in my one-track mind.

Beverly Whitney stepped out the front door promptly at a quarter to eight looking very professional in a brown pantsuit, nicely polished sensible shoes with low heels, carrying a legal assistant's briefcase. At the same moment a taxi pulled by to pick her up, acting out a precisely scheduled morning routine. The cab pulled away, no doubt in the direction of Fuller's office, and I continued my wait.

Spying on Castor, I discovered, consisted mostly of waiting for him to get up in the morning. By eleven he would usually appear and walk to the corner of Loudon for a paper, take a path through an empty lot to the back of a parking area, and then over to the coffee shop at the Mall. I followed on foot, close enough to see that he was tall with deep-set dark blue eyes, high cheek bones, and a generous display of carefully groomed black hair. He strolled with the pace of a man deep into daydreams. Kathy had told me that he was an aspiring actor, and even from a distance I could see he had an overload of the requisite style, but his pace suggested he wasn't aspiring too hard. He spent an hour or so over coffee, while I spent an hour or so outside the coffee shop trying to blend in with a garbage can. After he finished the coffee, Castor walked the ten blocks down Main Street to the The Ajax, the only legitimate theatre in town The Ajax was an old

Loews movie house that died when the Cineplex opened. I spent the afternoon on foot chasing after him. Well, chasing is not the right word, for the actor wannabe did everything at half speed. I strolled a block behind Castor while he visited The Ajax to check on upcoming auditions, back to the Mall where he bought the latest and tightest jeans, and to the market. He was the food shopper; I wondered who did the cooking. My sleuthing day finished after Castor carried his purchases home and no doubt settled in for a nap until Beverly returned.

◆   ◆   ◆

Thursday, the second day of this exciting work, brought more of the same, except he was toting a backpack. I noticed that he went for coffee at the same time and to the same diner. He took the same seat next to the window. After the hour-long coffee break, Castor strolled back to The Ajax, and then disappeared into a side door. The theatre was closed, but a sign advertised auditions for an upcoming production. I pushed open the exit door, snuck into the back of the auditorium where a few curious on-lookers were scattered about, and slid into a seat. A director, a producer, and a couple of assistants were seated about ten rows back from the stage. An actor was sweating and stammering out some lines. They were allowed to choose the lines they were best at, but the first two reminded me of my high school play. I was the villain because the other tall kid was the football quarterback who needed to be the hero. Castor was standing stage left, now sporting a Elizabethan jacket right out of the 16th Century. He strode

to the center, announced he was going to perform Hamlet's
'Speak the Speech.' Seemed a clever choice, trying out for a
part by performing a speech that told actors what to do. He
was good. I left before the jury gave its verdict—didn't Hamlet get poisoned?—and waited across the street. A half hour
later I tailed Castor back to the Mall where he spent some
time hanging around the magazine rack in the bookstore before stepping outside to make a couple of calls on his cell. He
took a detour through the rear parking lot. It was pretty deserted; I stayed back to keep from being spotted. He walked
to the far corner of the lot and leaned against a dumpster and
I hid behind a van and watched him through the windows.
An old taxi moved slowly through the lot, pulled up beside
Castor, and rolled down the window. There was a quick ex-
change. Too bad I wasn't working for the narcotics squad; I
could make an easy bust, mess up Castor's life a bit, and get
paid for it. Then I realized that I wasn't the only one watching the deal. A massive pea-green SUV was sitting across the
lot with someone at the wheel. He must have been waiting
there before we showed up. Looked to me like the narcs were
familiar with Castor's daily route and had parked there to
wait for him. The dealer put his taxi back in gear and drove
off and Castor disappeared down the path leading to Loudon
Street. The SUV began moving in my direction. I stayed behind the van as he passed, then stepped out far enough to see
the back of a round head. It was balanced on a pair of large
shoulders with no neck to intervene. His hair looked like it
was cut by the Marines and his ears spread out to the side
like short wave antennas. He looked more like a thug than a
narc, but that distinction was often unclear. I was waiting for

him to go after the pot merchant, but he drove out through the opposite exit. I stood alone, in the back corner of a bleak parking lot, wondering what the hell I just witnessed.

Realizing I'd lost my subject, I walked quickly towards Loudon, but Castor had already reached his house with most of the afternoon still before him. No doubt the weed would help him pass the time until Beverly arrived. Another day finished following a man who seemed to be totally unaware of what went on around him.

◆   ◆   ◆

On Friday I gambled that he would stick to his routine. I slept in. At 10:30 I drove directly to the diner, got there before Castor and found a booth where I could get a closer look and enjoy my coffee hot for a change. Sure enough, Castor popped in on time with a friendly smile, a 'good morning' to the waitress, and a wave to the guy behind the counter. She brought him his coffee and an apple Danish without his asking. Maybe she was charmed by his good looks, the kind that would photograph well, and perhaps the cucumber he had stuffed in his jeans also had a salutary effect; the cucumber that Kathy was a bit too familiar with. During my third cup of coffee, his cell phone chirped with some theme from "Cats" and he dug it out of his pocket. Castor's expression changed. This was apparently not a call from Dad for he held the cell close and lowered his voice. He'd done the drug deal yesterday, now something else was being planned. I moved to the register and fumbled with my change, stalling and over-hearing just "Monday" and a goodbye with a lot of "loves" attached. That was reason enough for me to give up the chase until Monday. I found the right change and left my target digging through the movie reviews.

7

A CRASH COURSE IN finance was in order. As Castor's house was not far from the town center and I remembered JJ's suggestion, I thought I'd check in on Doctor Dollar, aka Henry Cadman, financial consultant, trader, deal-maker, and all around money man. Mr. Cadman had the bad fortune to be my investment counselor, handling my retirement funds. Every Christmas he bought himself a couple of pairs of new argyle socks with the commissions he made from managing my portfolio. We'd known each other since college days, and he let friendship get in the way of good judgment and kept me on. The Doctor had an office in the sterile cube that sat next to the courthouse. I dropped by. He was busy, as usual, with a bevy of clients sitting in his waiting room. I sweet-talked the pretty and bored receptionist into telling me that at lunch he grabbed a sandwich and escaped to a City Hall Park bench whenever the weather allowed. As it was a fine crisp fall day, I crossed to the park to stake claim to a seat.

City Hall Park didn't attract many of the professionals who worked around it, they preferred power lunches; and the poor and the meek who came by to hang out were ejected by the local constabulary. I settled into an empty bench shaded by a bronze statue of some guy on a horse who had sacrificed enough of his troops to deserve a monument. I leaned back, enjoying the last days of the autumn sun. The days were getting shorter, the sun lower in the sky, and soon it wouldn't be high enough to peek over the courthouse at noon and warm the benches. I thought of the time when this Park must have been idyllic, the best of small town design, before the sides had been chopped off to make room for progress and the automobile. But then it would have reeked of horse manure and the smell of black smoke from old coal stoves. I was absentmindedly gazing at a fat pigeon who was gazing at me, when I noticed a couple leisurely walking along the other side of the street. Charming, I thought, until I realized it was Kathy and Muscles Corbutt. They walked in step, too close for my comfort, and the big guy kept touching her shoulder as they talked. And how beautifully she moved, and how she laughed as she spoke, no doubt reliving the evening before, remembering the soft lights, the wine over an intimate dinner she had prepared at her place, how they'd got a little high, and then Corbutt moved closer and Kathy said she was going to change into something more comfortable, and Corbutt . . . .

"Thinking of the millions I'm making for you in the market?" The voice of Henry Cadman broke in, just in time.

"Yes," I recovered quickly. "I was wondering when you'll get me enough to retire on. A nice little pension, a house in Tuscany, just a couple of servants."

Doctor Dollar was hugged by a tan suit that he'd bought before adding twenty-five pounds and three inches to his waist line. A green tie threatened to choke him, and if his brown belt snapped, buttons and zippers would be flying all over the lawn. He was a workaholic, sharp with the numbers and a terrific financial adviser, but he was cursed with a conscience which kept him from getting as rich as the ambitious MBA's in his office. One day something inside him was going to come unraveled. He treasured a solitary lunch break to calm his nerves, and here I was, sitting on his bench with a pocketful of questions.

"Johnny, I hate to tell you this, but a basic rule of the market is that you have to put something in to get something out. You haven't exactly been throwing money at me lately. Do you have some good news? Can you give me something to work with?" I think the Doctor really did worry about my finances.

"Actually, I need info."

"Again," he sighed. He parked himself on the bench beside me and opened a lunch bag.

"I'm doing a bit of undercover work for George Fuller, Fuller Investments. Know him?"

"George, yes. Strange dude. Seems out of place in the tight-assed financial business. Here, have something to eat. You could use a little fattening up." He handed me half of his tuna fish sandwich, and pointed to a wrapper full of pickle slices. "Fuller does all right though. I think his clients trust him because he doesn't fit the mold. Has a reputation for honesty. He'll stick with a client and do his level best to make the guy some money."

"Is he staying afloat? Business is good?" I asked.

"Rumor has it that he was pretty heavily into the mortgage market, and you know what happened to that. He's clearly in trouble."

"What about Whitney and Whitney?" I asked.

"Whitney? Now there's the opposite of Fuller. Very professional. Hard as nails. Gets what he wants. Made a bunch of money as an estate lawyer for the very rich. Picks up big commissions and invests it all, hedge funds, whatever. I can't say that I always like his methods, but he's big time, at least around here, in this small-time town. That's his building behind me, the town house on the corner. Here." He held out a bag of chips. "Does that satisfy your curiosity, or do you want a crash course in the market?"

"A crash course in mergers will suffice. Let's just suppose that Whitney and Fuller wanted to get together, merge companies."

"No need to be coy. It's common knowledge in my world. It has to be approved though, and that's the rub. But Whitney gives a lot of money to the pols. He might be able to pull some strings to get the approval."

"So why would Whitney be interested in Fuller Investments, especially if they're skating on thin ice?"

"As I said," the Doctor went on, "Fuller's reputation for honesty has convinced a few high rollers to rely on him. It's possible that Whitney wants to get his hands on them."

"How does this merger thing work?"

Doctor Dollar took a big bite out of his sandwich and started to explain, sending out equal bits of information and tuna fish. "Companies can merge if they want. Generally that's no problem. It's mostly routine paper work, and tax stuff, a pain in the ass, but not hard to do. But this case has been around since the summer, so something is holding it up. I figure they're waiting for approval."

"Approval, from where?" I asked.

"Well, it could be the Department of Justice, it could be the Federal Trade Commission, or it might be they've got an outside arbiter, could be . . . ."

I was getting frustrated with the legal swamp. "You're the expert, Doc. What's the law say about this merger? What's the bottom line?"

"Blue, sometimes you surprise me. You really think that it's all cut and dried and laid out in nice clear bold-faced legal print. You've got a combination of naiveté and cynicism that rivals the ladyboys of Thailand," Doc said without thinking.

"The who, what? The ladyboys? How do you know these things?" The Doc had surprised me again.

It was the first time I'd seen him blush, and he turned redder than a sunset over a Pittsburg steel mill. "Ah, oops, well," he stuttered. "You know I spend half my day on the web, and you should see the stuff they spam at you—can't get away from it."

"I know," I teased. "You're searching the web to buy a nice comfortable chair, you type in Lazy Boy, you make one little mistake and look what pops up. Whattya gonna do?"

"Damn it, Blue! I was looking up mergers."

"They're better off live, between two people. Now if you want to get a ladyboy involved . . . ."

"Will you shut up!" the Doc yelled. "Now, where was I? Oh yeah. The world of regulation in the financial markets is pretty fucked up." He paused. "A better word would be *eviscerated*. You'd think there'd be a set procedure to look at mergers, but the laws have been written by the corporations, and the last thing they want is visibility." He dropped into a style he no doubt used in teaching his kids about the birds and the bees. "First, there's the Anti-Trust Division of the Justice Department. They're interested in preventing monopolies that would limit competition. Then there's the FTC, the Federal Trade Commission. It can also get involved if it looks like there's a problem."

"But this should be small potatoes, no? Why would anyone care?" I asked.

The Doc chewed for a minute, then said, "I suspect that someone, I don't know who, has asked for a LOV."

"What's love got to do with it?"

"LOV, a Letter of Opinion of Value. The merger was suggested and somebody apparently has thrown up a red flag, so the powers that be need an approval. They can assign the job to someone in their office—a lawyer, or a judge, or an accountant for example—or they can contract outside with some auditing firm. Excuse me, are you listening?"

I was focusing on a woman who had just emerged from Whitney's building. "Doc, did you ever see such an angel?"

Twisting to peer over his shoulder: "I can barely see that far. What have you got—some kind of sensor that beeps whenever it picks up estrogen within a hundred yards?" Doc impatiently stuffed the remains of his lunch into a paper bag. "I haven't got all day, let's leave the sex and get back to the LOV. Is the process clear?"

I nodded. "Sure, it's clear as a bell. Whitney and Fuller want to merge, and started the process a couple of months ago. Should have been routine, but somebody, we don't know who, has said there might be a problem here. So the DOJ or the FTC has asked for an LOV. Now somebody, we don't know who, is looking into it and may or may not approve it, sooner or later. Couldn't be clearer."

"Exactly!" Doctor Dollar was pleased. "Cookie? Cindy made 'em, and I get whatever doesn't fit it my kid's lunch box."

"Just one more thing, Doc, if you could."

Henry winced.

"Well if someone has to okay it, that probably means it's a public document and you could see it. Right?"

"Don't know if it's public, but I suspect I could get my hands on it." The Doctor reluctantly agreed. "I might have to call in a couple of favors."

"Could you check it out, just see what you can find? And I'm wondering who gets to give it the seal of approval?"

"What's in it for me?" sighed the Doctor.

"The usual," I said. "Need someone to follow your wife around and see who she's shacking up with and I'm your man. Free of charge."

"Great. How could I turn down an offer like that?"

"Look at it this way. You need my services, they're free. You don't need them, that's good for you. You win both ways."

"Sorry, Blue, you can't get away with that. If somebody wins, someone else loses. Life is a zero-sum game."

◆ ◆ ◆

A lot of the Doctor's explanation had fallen into the root cellar at the bottom of my brain, but one thing was clear: some official had to approve the merger and Whitney would be laying on the pressure. I decided I'd rather think about sipping a martini on my terrace. Well, fire escape, but there was enough room for a chair and an egg-crate footstool. I leaned back, put my feet up, and took the first sip. From the back of The Arms the ground sloped down, stretched over a field of uncut brush to the old railroad-yards. Evening had arrived—the warm red light of the sunset washed over the tracks—rows of tracks, rusting, mostly unused. A locomotive moved slowly in the distance, pushing a boxcar into place, assembling a freight train. The second martini, combined with the financial mumbo-jumbo, restarted a dream I have of becoming a hobo, walking the tracks and jumping a slow-moving freight. No cares, no direction, no Gods and no goals. A dream I never really worked out in much detail like, where would I get a slice of pizza and a beer and are there any girl hobos? 'Girl?' That's not correct. *Female* hobos? *Women* hobos? How about the Latin term hoba—plural, hobae? I wonder if I could find any nice hobae out there. It was getting late. I'd solved the hobo-hoba problem. I'd work on the pizza and beer problem tomorrow. As for the rest of the weekend, maybe I'll call Kathy. Or maybe I won't.

8

SATURDAY MORNING. THE PHONE woke me at an hour when working men thought everybody should be up. It was Chief Inspector JJ Cakes, following up on the job he had mentioned. A Judge Plumworth has asked him to stop by to talk about police protection for a big shindig he's throwing for the Governor and he wants to make sure there are no surprises. JJ thinks there may be work in it for me, as an undercover presence at the party. Something is obviously troubling the Judge, for he feels the necessity to go beyond the normal security procedures. JJ said he'd pick me up at nine, and told me not to keep him waiting. He had a good memory.

I showered, shaved, and rummaged through the closet for a nicely fitted black suit jacket. I knew that a sharp-looking outfit gave the impression of rich and smart. People like rich—I'm not so sure about smart. Picked out a pressed white shirt, no tie, and gave my black loafers a once-over with the brush. Combed my hair to one side and wondered if I should keep the stud in my ear. Decided against it.

JJ rang the buzzer at 9:01 sharp. He was looking very professional in a crisply pressed uniform and a shiny blue-and-white squad car. He filled me in on the Judge's history as we drove over. Plumworth was a Judge in the County Court and now under consideration for a position on the State District Court. JJ went on: "I've known the family for years. Somehow I seem to be the cop that's always called in for the scandals. I think the Judge trusts me. Anyway, like I said, he called yesterday and wants to talk about police for a party he's giving next week. The Governor will be the guest of honor and he doesn't want anything to go wrong. That's routine, but he also received a veiled threat about a case he's working on, and he thinks it would be wise to have some plainclothes hanging around. That's where you could be useful. He's a good chap, the Judge. Fair in the court but a bit helpless when it comes to the personal stuff."

"What else should I know?" I encouraged JJ to go on.

"He married early on, but there were troubles from the start. His wife was a spoiled heir of the Bertrand fortune, and probably was playing around on the side. In and out of the gossip columns. It only lasted a few years though; she died in childbirth. That must have been over twenty-some years ago. But I think he'd sell the kids just to be able get that judgeship, and the Governor is the guy who decides."

We drove through the posh Pine Tree Heights and turned on to Elm Drive. It had always been popularly known as Millionaire's Row, a spotlessly clean macadam lane that wound through an area of luxurious estates rivaling any on the East Coast. This row, however, was a bit left over: old money housing older families. Most of the younger generation had gone to the Ivies, graduated, and moved into condos in the city, and now made money from money. The roadway was lined and in some places completely covered with the large fast-growing maples that moved in when the blight took out the stately elms. Winding along the Drive, we passed high stone walls and caught glimpses of Tudor giants, which disappeared again into the shamelessly over-painted fall leaves. JJ turned the squad car into a driveway between two huge granite gateposts. We passed a small gatehouse, built with the same rock. It looked lived in—some well-tended flowers were the giveaway. The Plumworth Mansion materialized before us like Scarlett O'Hara's Tara when the moon emerged from behind the clouds.

The graveled driveway circled around a fountain with a glorious group of naked white marble muses in the center. The pool was dry and water no longer poured over marble skin. The grounds were well groomed, the lawns and gardens were clean and manicured, but the stables appeared to be empty and the outbuildings no longer in use. The Mansion was built of stone and framed by two rounded turrets. An aggressive ivy was doing its best to climb to the top, hanging on with tentacles digging into the mortar, and cut away only around each deep-set window. A wide array of steps led to a slate terrace that extended along the front and around both sides. Large-leafed hydrangeas grew from waist-high ceramic pots. A low marble railing wrapped around the outside of the terrace setting off a stately space where a duke and duchess could have strolled comfortably.

"It was the wife's money, this bungalow," JJ continued. "She died giving birth to the twins, Sonny and Helen. Left a strange will giving the entire estate to Sonny. And what a helluvan estate—couple of hundred million. Sonny's in charge of the money and the Mansion. Rich Sonny Plumworth. He lets his father, the Judge, stay here, and dribbles out a few dollars to his sister when he feels like it. He still lives here; so does Helen. She stays at the gatekeeper's cottage we just passed. Probably gives her a bit of distance." I could see JJ was not too fond of the place.

A few steps up from the terrace was an impressive wooden door that looked as though it were made from the last of the elm trees. We couldn't find a bell, and I was looking forward to swinging the brass knocker when the door creaked open and a butler appeared. In the old days he would have been a full-time butler, but in these times he's a butler, gardener, work crew, garbage man, and general handyman from somewhere south of the border. I named him Higgins. Higgins led us into a two-story-high marble foyer, centering on a wide curving staircase designed to enhance the grand entrance of the belle of the ball. We followed him through a pair of doors on the left side of the entrance hall to a large living room. "Wait here, please."

We were in a cavernous Victorian room. Heavy drapes, plush cushioned couches, a sea of deep-red carpeting and dark walnut molding. A bearskin lay on the floor, head and all, looking like it wanted to bite a chunk out of my foot. Heads of a large-antlered moose and a leopard stuck out of the wallpaper. The obligatory gun cabinet stood by the door filled with an assortment of gaming rifles and shotguns, and a few pistols that looked like they were handed down through a couple of generations. It was more for show than actual use, although, like any typical gumshoe, I did wonder who in the household held the permits. An ornamental chandelier hung overhead and there were some large portraits of distinguished bearded gentlemen staring out between the dead animals, and some Hudson River School paintings which probably were worth buckets of gold coins. The frames certainly were. The room centered on an oversized fireplace. A full-length portrait of a young couple hung over the mantlepiece.

"The Judge and his wife," volunteered JJ.

"There should be some trophies."

A young woman bounced in on heels that were high enough to strengthen her pelvic floor muscles. She looked familiar, but I wasn't much good at remembering faces. Thin, taut, and almost pretty with closely cropped hair that must have been trimmed in the last half hour. Tall, I think, or maybe it was the effect of the ankle-breaker heels. A tight blue skirt to her knees enforced the short, quick steps. A matching buttoned blouse was fitted to define the term 'perky.' Her breasts chatted between themselves for a moment, nudged each other, and then decided to let JJ in. "You can come in now," she said pointedly to JJ. The detective nodded toward me, but the secretary shook her head. "It's better he waits here."

JJ knew which way to go, and he disappeared following the heels through a door with the official plaque: "Plumworth Legal Offices." I was left to waste some time in the living room making believe I had just returned from an African safari.

9

I SETTLED INTO A large armchair and tried to get interested in last year's copy of the *Harvard Law Review*. I skimmed over articles on famous Harvard grads, each wrapped comfortably in admiring quotations. Apparently anyone who mattered had a graduation year hanging off the back of their name like a fuzzy rabbit's tail. I sat back into the plush cushions thinking I could get used to this. I lit up a fat Havana cigar, flicked the match into the fireplace, rang for the butler. He'd know to bring me my favorite single malt scotch with two ice cubes. I'd offer her one when she arrived, and maybe go for a drive in the country in my silver and gold Aston Martin convertible. She appeared, and looked me over. I could see that small talk was not going to be necessary. It was a hot, steamy day, and she was wearing . . . .

The sharp click of high heels interrupted my brief journey into the good life, and marked the reappearance of the Judge's secretary. She crossed the room like a hungry warbler, her eyes darting here and there to find any signs of food or something out of place that she could set right.

"I'm sorry. I didn't get your name," she chirped.

"Heron, Johnny Heron," I replied. "But my friends call me . . . ."

"My apologies, Mr. Heron. I didn't mean to be un-friendly, but the Judge told me he wanted to speak to In-spector Cakes and didn't mention anyone else. I hope you don't mind waiting." She rearranged every item on the cof-fee table as she spoke, positioning the magazines, the ash tray, and the lighter so that each was the same distance from the other, and from the table's edge.

"You work here?" I asked, for lack of anything else to say.

"Yes. Secretary, assistant, advisor, whatever is called for."

I rolled the 'whatever is called for' over in my mind.

"Sorry, I didn't introduce myself," she went on. "Irene Wiseman."

"Glad to meet you, Miss Wiseman." She bobbed her head, turned, and disappeared back through the door to the Judge's office, straightening the sign on the door as she went in. I reached down and pushed the magazines around—too much order is never a good thing—and tried to restart the Aston Martin. I managed to get my lady friend dressed in a micro-mini and into the front seat when my concentration was broken by the approaching voices of a man and a woman—angry voices. The couple didn't see me and the fight continued into the room. He was spitting curses like a sailor and treating her like a child although they looked the same age. In fact, I'd say they could be twins. They were both slender, she a bit taller than he and very beautiful. He had the same blond hair but with a crew cut that I thought went out with the fifties. She was designed by a perfectionist with an imagination: thin, tall, blond hair to her shoulders, blue eyes with long lashes. She was wearing a loose-fitting blue blouse, mostly buttoned; a pleated skirt, short but not too short; and no shoes. Her fingers were long and inviting, with nails that could damage a back if one was lucky enough to get to know her. He had the same perfect features, but on him the result was an unsettling picture. Each part was set just a bit out of place. His ears and mouth were stuck on like a grown-up version of Mr. Potato Head. The nose was tilted in a direction which changed depending on which way he faced, and it was impossible to tell exactly where he was looking. Each limb moved as though it was in competition with the others, leaving a picture of someone who didn't know where he was going and was intensely aware of it.

He was berating her about some, as he saw it, unnecessary expense, going on about how difficult it was for him to watch over every dollar and how she should shape up and grow up. She let him have a "Fuck off, you pervert!"

He sputtered, "You little bitch," and moved threateningly toward her.

I stood up just as he raised his hand for a hard slap. "No, I'm afraid that wouldn't be a good idea."

"Don't tell me what to do, and who the fuck are you anyway?" He spat the words in my direction.

I didn't really have a good answer for that, so I said nothing.

She turned toward me. "Are you a client?" Marlene Dietrich came to mind first, and then in quick succession Nicole Kidman, Yvette Mimieux, and Mata Hari. I actually have no idea what Mata Hari looked like, but I knew she was inscrutable and exotic.

"You're here to see my father?" she asked again. Looking directly at me, or more accurately, directly into me as though she was downloading information from the hard drive in my brain.

"I don't give a shit who you are," chimed in Mr. Potato Head. "You're outta here, or I call the cops."

"Actually, I am the cops. Chief Inspector Cakes is with the Judge now."

The nameless blond angel looked concerned. "What's wrong? Is anything wrong?"

"I think it's a business meeting," I said. Then thinking that didn't sound too upright for a judge, "He's just getting filled in on some police procedure."

I was getting to Potato Head; he was clenching his fists and getting redder by the minute. His macho had been pricked and he was ready to hit somebody. Figuring it was better me than her, I stepped between them. "Look I'm just waiting here. Waiting here till Cakes comes out. Then I go, not before, okay?" I was bigger than he was—a good four inches taller, twenty pounds heavier—and he didn't know what a lousy fighter I was.

"You'll pay, you prick!" He half swallowed the words, turned and left, trying not to stomp on the way out.

Mata Hari, the blond spy, looked into me again. "You're a private eye," she stated rather than asked.

"Yes, that's one name for it, but is it so obvious?"

"Of course," she laughed. "Just look at the shoes."

I did. They were just my black loafers. "What's wrong with the shoes . . . ?"

Her laugh was warm and friendly. I was entranced and tried to explain. "Yes, but I'm here helping JJ with some police work. Used to have a real job down at the precinct."

"Sure," she said, as though she believed about half of the statement. "I hope you find what you came for." I had the feeling that she could easily have done my work for me and put me out of a job. She waited a moment and then said, "Why don't we share a coffee? Come, the kitchen's through here." I followed her through the swinging doors that led to the kitchen. Even bare-footed she moved as though on wheels, gliding into and about the kitchen—a ballet entitled "Making Coffee," with a rapt audience of one. I should have kept my mouth shut, but I was a private dick.

"Why 'pervert'?"

"What?"

"'Pervert.' The word carries a lot of weight."

Her answer startled me. It was a response so candid that it would have taken weeks to dig up the same amount of dirt. "Oh, he's planking Whizzie, my dad's pretend secretary but real paramour. Pretty lousy, don't you think?"

"That's what the fight was about? Whizzie?"

"No, this one was about money, the last one was Whizzie, before that . . . ." She trailed off.

"Whizzie—where does someone come up with that?" I assumed it was a nickname drawn from Wiseman when she was three years old and couldn't object. I was trying to lighten the tone.

"She appeared a year or more ago and put the make on Dad. She did help him get through a rough time. He had a pretty shaky heartbeat back then. Has a pacemaker and a history of heart problems, but I think her care won him over. He's a pushover, but she's really thinking of the Mansion; that's as clear as cut glass."

She stood with her back toward me, preparing the coffee, while I was trying to come up with a name for the color of her toenail polish.

"Seduction Blue," she said without even turning around. "Bought it in Italy, can't find it anymore. Find me some and I'll give you a reward." She laughed mischievously. "Milk, sugar, or unadulterated private-eye black?"

"Lots of milk and sugar," I answered honestly, effectively undercutting my tough image.

The goddess handed me the cup. She sat opposite me while we sipped the coffee, at first a bit casually, but then she moved her knees together and turned her toes in. The attempt at the teen-age model look wasn't very convincing.

"You were downtown yesterday," I said.

She studied me, waiting for an explanation.

"Coming out of the office of Whitney and Whitney."

"How do you know?"

"I was in the park. You're hard to miss, Ms. Plumworth."

"Helen, please."

"How well do you know Mr. Whitney, Helen?" The Helen didn't sound right. I wanted to say 'sweety' or 'darling,' but then I thought of Helen of Troy and the name and the figure before me became one.

"Yes I do. Douglas Whitney has been around the family for a long time, helps my dad's campaigns among other things. I'm sure he hopes to get a favor or two, but that's normal. Anyway, I'd like to get my fair share of the estate, so I made a deal with him."

"I gather the will gives everything to your brother. Does Whitney thinks he can change that?"

"Everything goes to the eldest. Sonny came out before me so he got it all. We were obviously conceived at the same time and then born less than a minute apart, so the idea of the eldest gets a bit fuzzy. Whitney thinks he can challenge the will and get me half."

"And Whitney gets a big cut if he can do that?"

"Of course. You know that's the way it works." Helen hesitated, then said, "You don't like him very much, do you?"

"Let's just say he picked me up on a blind date and it didn't work out."

Helen laughed. "Mr. Whitney tends to get what he wants. If you're in the way, good luck."

We sat quietly. She seemed to drift into a daydream and I was hoping it included me. I drifted into a daydream and it certainly included her. The silence was broken by the voices of JJ and the Judge in the living room—I'd have to finish the dream later.

"I should go," I said.

We set down the empty cups and I followed Helen into the living room. The Judge was the gray-haired version of the man in the painting. Dressed neatly, he was a man who would wear a coat and tie twenty-four hours a day. Helen went up to her father and tenderly took his arm. He thanked JJ and nodded to me. Spending time on the bench teaches you not to be too friendly.

Helen looked at me. "Thank you. Come by sometime. I'm in the gatehouse."

I smiled. I actually thought she meant it.

10

EARLY MONDAY MORNING AND the sun was thinking about getting up. I arrived at Castor's place and parked in my usual spot under the sycamore tree. It had only been three days but it was enough time for most of the leaves to have fallen to the street. They lay under the car, and the tree stood quite naked. Beverly Whitney opened the front door on schedule at a quarter to eight, but today Cass was right behind her. She was in her business suit carrying the usual attaché case, and he was in his uniform jeans and a polo shirt, the casual playboy. Castor's BMW was parked by the curb. They climbed in and he started down the street. The cup holder on my old Honda had long since broken, so I tucked the hot coffee between my legs, waited until they turned the corner, put the Honda in gear, pulled away from the curb, and followed about a block behind. I had to step on the gas to keep up once I realized that the only thing Castor did that was not at a leisurely pace was drive. We were moving against the morning traffic and I had trouble keeping the BMW in sight. Cass tore through town heading for the east side, treating stop signs as though they were only suggestions. I began to worry about spilling the coffee, then remembered a case a couple of years ago where a woman picked up a steaming hot coffee at a McDonalds' drive-in window, and it fell over in her lap as she drove away. The coffee was scalding! She suffered some bad burns, sued the Golden Arches, won, and was awarded about a million bucks. Maybe I should try that. I'm standing in the court and the Judge has ruled in my favor, and he has to come up with a figure for the settlement. I'm trying to get a grip on the dollar value of my gonads, when I turn a corner and damn near rear-end Castor. He had actually stopped at a red light. Screeching to a halt inches from his back bumper only prompted him to wave a finger out the window, and then speed away. I followed him into the Pine Tree Heights area, and the next thing I knew he was on Millionaire's Row. This fancy part of town was beginning to feel like home. I dropped back a bit more. The traffic was light in the elite area at this time of the morning, and I didn't want to be spotted. Around a couple of turns and up ahead, the Judge's Mansion appeared. The BMW pulled between the pillars and came to a stop in the curved driveway. I was here yesterday working for JJ; now I'm here today working for Fuller. My two jobs were overlapping and it didn't make much sense. I left my car a bit down the road, walked to the gate, and stood behind one of the granite posts. I didn't know what was in the cards, but a sleuth's job is mostly waiting to find out, and maybe I would be rewarded with a glimpse of Helen. Bev was out of the car, up the stairs, and I caught sight of Higgins through the door as she entered. She's a legal assistant; this is a Judge's mansion and sometimes office. I'm assuming there's some connection.

Castor didn't wait. He started the car and was coming down the driveway. I was hiding behind the pillar thinking what an idiot I was to leave my car. He turned onto the lane and there was no chance I would catch up with him, but he drove about a hundred yards and then pulled over to the side. It was an odd place to wait for Beverly, a spot out of sight of the Mansion. A door opened and closed directly behind me and I flattened myself against the stone as Helen glided by, not five feet away. She seemed unaware of the Fall chill, and was wearing a loose summer dress that tried to keep up with her. Over that a magenta drapery struggled to prevent some of her parts from immodestly escaping. Carrying a small suitcase, she walked straight to the BMW, got in, and they started off. Cass had been waiting for Helen, not Beverly!

I was spying from behind the pillar, and someone was watching me from behind the hedge. I turned in time to see a head drop out of sight, but being more interested in keeping track of the couple than in running down the Peeping Tom, I ignored him and ran back to my car. Trying to pick up speed, I sprayed gravel around the Mansion lawn, hopefully a bit on Mr. Spy. By the time I reached the end of Millionaire's Row, Castor had a pretty good lead. Tailing people, especially through traffic, isn't as easy as it looks in the movies. There are annoyances like slow drivers, traffic regulations, pedestrians, and a familiar pea-green SUV that cut me off and left me at a stop light. I had to wait for a few cars to go through, then I ran the light and broke some other laws trying to catch up. I did catch sight of them up ahead as they headed north out of town, but some garbage truck did me in when he stopped to do his thing. Damn! What kind of a private eye can't even find a way to get around a garbage truck. I did get some satisfaction when No-Neck in his SUV passed me in the other direction. Castor's heavy foot must have also left him behind.

◆   ◆   ◆

I pulled over and thumbed Fuller's number into my cell. "Mr. Fuller, Heron here. I've spotted the Jezebel and she and Cass have gone off together."

"Tell me!" He didn't sound amused. "What do you know?"

"You're sure you want me to continue on this. I've been in this business long enough to realize that this kind of stuff, dirt, usually isn't worth finding out. Solves nothing and generally makes the situation worse. Your son and the woman seem pretty close at the moment. I'd advise you sit back and let it play itself out and hope he comes home. What other choice have you got?"

"Don't lecture me, Heron. Just, ah, give me what you're paid for."

"She's about 23, gorgeous, and they've just driven off to somewhere up north, with more than an overnight bag."

Fuller swore. "Damn! He's headed up the coast for an actor's workshop and has taken her along. He's supposed to be there all week. I want to know where they're going, ah, staying. You can do that, yes?"

"You give me the name of the workshop and I'm your man." Fuller gave me the details. I always wondered what they did at actor's workshops and I was going to get a chance to find out. It would take a few hours to drive up the coast, enough of a reason to put it off until tomorrow.

It was an unusual Monday for me; I'm starting a week holding two jobs, there's a puzzle to solve, pretty women to follow, and money coming in. Maybe I could get used to this and give up on my idea of running off with a hoba. But, then again . . . .

11

THE DRIVE UP THE coast was familiar. I remembered it from college days driving with friends and beer, although I couldn't remember if there was any reason we headed that way, except for the beer. It varied between Atlantic Ocean coastline, small towns, and strip development. The towns were once charming but now each had been gutted in the center to make room for a new gas station and drive-in bank. The commercial strips, one of America's finest inventions, filled the spaces between the towns and kept the traffic moving at a speed hospitable to shopping. Oldies from the 50's poured out of my radio—I kept the adrenaline flowing by bopping to Bill Haley and the Comets. The only time and place where I could sing out loud was when I was alone inside a moving car. Truck drivers who pulled alongside hoping to catch a glimpse of a hiked-up skirt were treated to a madman jawing and bouncing to a silent beat. About half way up the coast 40,000 watts of God began talking over the Big Bopper. I drove the last half in silence.

Fuller's directions were good, and I pulled up to the gate of an old getaway hotel. It was now home to anything that would pay the rent, and this week it was pretending to be an actor's workshop. The guy sitting at the entrance didn't have that cynical suspicion that pervades us city folk and was eager to chat. The workshop had finished for the day—pretty easy hours I thought—so he looked up Castor Fuller in the register. Cass wasn't staying there but was lodged up the shore a bit. 7 Sunset Lane was written in the book. My new friend said he thought it was near a village called New Troy about five miles up the coast, near the cliffs that rose above the beach. We talked a bit about the cold spell and how the politicians in Washington always screw everything up. I thanked him and headed off to search for the den of iniquity.

It took a drug store, a laundromat, and the local burger joint before I could get good directions. I think it was the first five-dollar tip the kid ever got for a double burger and fries, but it loosened him up. He plotted a route that would take me to Sunset Lane.

Not far from town, I convinced my Honda to tackle a rutted dirt road up a steep slope to the cliffs by the sea. The wind was stronger at this height, blowing off the shore where waves crashed on the rocks a couple hundred feet below. Ahead, a small weathered New England gray shingled cabin stood alone, with not a tree or shrub to give it protection from the wind. An old place, maybe a room and a half with a screened-in porch along the front. There was no indication that this was number seven, and I hadn't seen any sign of one through six on the way up, but Castor's car was parked in front. I slowly drove by. A couple was wrapped together on the porch swing so tightly that it was hard to tell where one began and the other left off, but Helen's blond hair was the giveaway. They were clearly the sinful pair. I wondered why Fuller was so curious about this place, but I had done my work. Nothing in my mission said there was any reason to disturb the love birds. I drove to the end of the lane, hung a U-turn and headed back down the coast. This detective stuff is pretty vapid at times, but it looked like I could gather my bucks and leave this case. I was already missing the chance to follow Helen around for a few more weeks.

◆   ◆   ◆

I was tired and not looking forward to the trip back, retracing the route down the coast to home to sleep, or maybe to drink and sleep, or maybe to drink, jack off, and sleep, or maybe all that in a different order. At times like these I'm happy to be living alone. It's hard to imagine someone putting up with me anyway.

Four hours later I turned the old Honda onto Machinist's Drive. I passed Iron, Inc., dark and deserted, but the lights of the Pharm-a-Lot retail store were still on. I had a few more minutes before it closed for the night, a few more minutes to pick up some sleeping pills. I pulled into the lot and parked next to the only other late-evening customer. That customer turned out to be Irene Wiseman. She was perched on her six-inch heels at the counter, her back to me.

"Good evening Ms. Wiseman," I said cheerily. "Not the kind of neighborhood I'd expect to see you in after dark."

She turned and looked blankly at me, without recognition at first. "Oh, you're the lawman who came with JJ to see the Judge. I'm picking up the Judge's meds. What brings you here?"

"I live here, down the road a bit." I suddenly remembered where I'd seen her before. "You used to work here, yes? On the other side of the counter." Her new job with the Judge was a pretty good step up the ladder.

"That was a couple of years ago." Whizzie quickly tucked the prescription into her purse and began to rearrange the candies on the counter while the clerk was cashing the hundred that she had given him.

"My place is not far away, and I've got some nice etchings," I said, trying to lighten the mood, and hell, it never hurts to try.

"It's a nice offer." Whizzie laughed nervously and picked up the change. "But I'm due back. Maybe another time." She clicked toward the door, the heels adding a lovely motion to her backside, gave me a brisk wave and she was gone.

♦ ♦ ♦

I started back along the potholed road by the familiar deserted warehouses. I was thinking that it wouldn't be so difficult to take a wheelbarrow full of tar out the front gate of the asphalt plant and fill a couple of the holes, when I noticed a pair of headlights turning after me. I was hoping Whizzie had decided to follow up on the etchings, but no luck. It looked like a small truck. I put some pressure on the Honda gas pedal—it still had a pretty good kick—but the headlights stayed behind me. I slowed down enough to be delivering newspapers. Sure enough, headlights stuck there, about a block back. I hung a right, a right, a right, and then back toward Dung Hill Arms, otherwise known as number 23. This guy had to be the worst tail ever—he followed me around the block. With that talent he didn't appear to be too dangerous. I pulled around to the side of the Arms and parked in my usual spot next to the deserted van. When I walked around front to the door, I could see him parked up the street. Lights off now, it looked like an old Toyota pick-up truck, with a license plate that was covered in mud. I started to walk toward it. I had closed about half the distance when the Toyota groaned to life, the brights came on, and it jerked forward. I thought maybe I could catch a glimpse of the amateur as he sped by, but the 'by' part wasn't happening. The pick-up was headed straight for me and whoever was piloting it had his foot hard on the accelerator. I guess I really didn't believe it and kept walking ahead, until I realized I was playing chicken with a ton and a half of steel. I'm not sure whether he swerved or not but I leapt into the thick barberry and briers that masqueraded as hedge and left a piece of my cuff on his back bumper.

"Fuck!"

I scrambled out of the prickles in time to see taillights disappear around the bend by the graveyard, then dragged myself back through the front door of the Arms. Javier looked up. I was pretty scratched up but, being Javier, he just said, "Good evening, Mr. Heron," and waited to see if anything else was called for. I ignored him and climbed the stairs to the third floor. There was some rubbing alcohol under the bathroom sink, and it stung like hell when I dabbed it on. My mother used to say that the sting meant the germs were dying. That never cheered me up—it just made me feel sorry for the germs. I poured out some real alcohol, thought it would be best to treat the wounds from both sides, inside and out. I downed a glass of warm vodka, sank into the armchair and decided to put the rest of the evening's plans on hold.

12

"WHAT CAN I DO for you?" Ms. Henry said in her best secretarial voice. "Mr. Fuller is quite busy right now."

"I think he'd like to talk with me," I said, and walked into his office, closing the door behind me.

Fuller really didn't look like he wanted to see me, but he gave a "hold the calls" over the intercom. Given the state of his business, I doubted there would be many calls to hold.

"Bring me up to date," he said wearily.

I gave a quick summary: "Cass and his girlfriend are hanging out in a small cottage up the coast, about five miles from the workshop. Last time I saw them they were all over each other on the front porch swing."

"7 Sunset Lane, right, yes?" Fuller surprised me with the address. I thought I was supposed to give that information to him.

"Yes," I went on. "A small coastal cottage all weathered with gray shingles. Sits on top of the cliffs, overlooking the ocean. Looks like it hasn't been lived in for a while. Not much around it."

"Okay, enough," growled Fuller. "I figured he'd use that place. I shouldn't have told him about it, but it seemed like he, ah, deserved to know."

"Know what, why?" He was doing a better job of private investigating than I was.

"Never mind!" Fuller shot back. "Just tell me what you know about the girl."

"She's a few years younger than Castor, very beautiful, lives in the rich section of town. I think Ms. Whitney has had some business dealings with her father. In fact it's possible that's how Castor met her in the first place."

Fuller perked up. "Her name?"

"Helen Plumworth. She's the daughter of a Judge Plumworth. Lives in a palatial estate over on Elm Drive."

Fuller's knee hit the table with a thud as he jerked upright. "Judge Plumworth! Are you sure?"

"Yes, I've been there, met him, met her. I'm sure. You know the Judge?"

"Well, sort of," Fuller mumbled. "Some business stuff." He fell silent.

"A problem? Should I know?" I prompted.

"No, nothing more, Heron. You've done your job. You're done. Give Ms. Henry your billing information on the way out, and the check is in the mail."

"All right. You're happy with my work?" I said before realizing that it was a pretty bad choice of words.

"Fine, just fine, and you're, ah, finished with it, right? You private eyes are supposed to do your stuff and then disappear, yes?" He said finally.

"Right."

"Good." Then, "Goodbye, Heron." Fuller was done with me now. He sat at his desk looking straight ahead. I don't know what was going through his brain, but it didn't look like he was composing Valentines. As I left I noticed that Marie Henry had moved away from the filing cabinet sooner this time, but she knew I was done here. She handed me a form with instructions to fill in dates, hours, expenses, social security number, address, etc. I sat in the only reception area chair and went to work, feeling as though I was applying for a job that had already been filled. In the next room I saw Beverly Whitney sitting in front of her computer and wondered how she reconciled working for Fuller after having been the cause of Whitney and Whitney and No Sons. Perhaps she also wondered about that as she was gazing into space, her thoughts miles away. I had only seen her from a distance before, but now, upon closer inspection, I saw that she could be beautiful. Hidden behind the legal facade was a pole dancer about to perform. The formality, the perfectly tailored suit, was hiding a body that was anxious to spring free. Beverly pushed the computer away, turned and started toward me, dropping the suit jacket off her shoulders and to the floor. By the time she entered the reception room, four buttons of her starched blouse were unbuttoned and she was working on the fifth, exposing a tight black push-up bra that threatened to toss her breasts into the air. I stood and . . . .

"Are you finished?" Ms. Henry asked, and then, "Thank you. I'll send everything along in the morning."

I started for the door and felt that Beverly was still getting to me, until I realized that the cell phone in my pants pocket was set on vibrate. I dug it out, checked the caller ID, and saw Henry Cadman's name pop up. Best not to answer that until I was outside.

As soon as I hit the street I called the good Doctor. Good timing. I was in need of an update on new developments in the merger business. "Good morning, Henry, how're they hanging?"

"Johnny, is that you?"

"Yep, afraid so. You called because you need me to check up on your wife?"

"Go to hell. I don't know why I deal with you. Yesterday I searched through the court records and was able to dig up a copy of the merger proposal. You might be interested. Can you drop by the Park at 12:30 tomorrow, the usual bench, and this time you bring the lunch."

"I'll be there."

Fuller had fired me and I should be done with this business. Sometimes the hardest part of my profession is knowing when to quit. I seldom got it right.

13

I WAS LATE, RUNNING down the hall, and I couldn't remember where the room was. I was at my desk. There was a test, in something. What class was this? Barbara Jane was giving me some papers. Barbara Jane Headly, the busty cheerleader who sat in front of me and got A's in everything, and she was pressed against me, and the damn class bell kept ringing. I was naked but no one seemed to care. If only that bell would stop. Doorbell, something in my mind was prompting: doorbell.

I sat up, awake enough to see ten o'clock on the wall. Thursday morning, the sun was fighting to get around the mostly pulled curtains. I stood up, naked, couldn't find any underpants so I grabbed the pair of jeans that was lying on the floor. Tugged them over a hard on, compliments of Barbara Jane. I had my shirt mostly buttoned when I opened the door to find a primly suited Beverly Whitney standing, finger poised to punch the bell again.

"Good morning, Mr. Heron. I hope I didn't wake you."

"No, no, of course not. Just getting ready to go to work." I fumbled, trying to surreptitiously zip up my fly.

"I'm sorry to bother, but . . . may I come in?" Ms. Whitney asked.

"Yes, please." I stepped aside. The perfectly trimmed Whitney walked in. I pulled open the drapes, tossed some newspapers off the couch and pointed to it. She placed her case on the floor, carefully smoothed her skirt beneath her, and sat on the edge of the couch as if she was afraid she might catch something from it. I suddenly was very aware of my bare feet and felt about as naked as I had been in the dream. "Maybe you would like a coffee?" I tried to be hospitable. Fortunately, she said no. Maybe she knew it would be two tablespoons of instant and a dollop of non-dairy creamer. I sat down on the chair opposite the couch, hid my feet under the coffee table, and waited.

"Mr. Heron . . . ," she began.

"John, please," I interrupted. "Or Blue if you wish. My friends call me Blue."

"Nice of you to think of me as a friend, Mr. Heron," she said, and settled back a bit more comfortably into the couch, crossing her legs, sliding nylon against nylon, creating the sound I had imagined. It made me aware that I still hadn't settled down inside my pants. "But really, this is a business meeting."

I waited. It was my best and possibly my only technique for keeping a conversation going.

"I know that Mr. Fuller hired you, and I figure it was probably about Cass." She surprised me.

"Why do you think that, Ms. Whitney?"

"Mr. Heron, I'm not that naïve. I know Cass has his affairs. And I know who this one is with. That's why I'm here."

"I can't really talk about it," I explained. "It's a private eye code of conduct. Not that we're known for having much in the way of scruples, but what I know has to stay confidential."

Beverly uncrossed her legs and crossed them the other way, and I suspected she was well aware of what she was doing to my rational mind. "You don't have to tell me anything. I'll do the talking," she went on. "Cass and I have not been doing that well for some time now, but we thought we'd hold off on any separation until after the all-important merger. You know my father and Mr. Fuller are trying to merge the two companies. We figured that a break-up might spook my father and squelch the deal."

"Doesn't sound like you're on such good terms with your pop." I took a guess.

"No, I'm not a son," Beverly said with surprising candor. "I'm the second half of Whitney and Whitney, the part that doesn't exist. I can work with Fuller, but I was never really able to get along in Father's firm. He's a hard man to work for. We're not on very good terms and there's just too much baggage to allow us to work together. After Mother left it was heavy going, and I moved over to Fuller's firm. It's been easier—I have a lot more freedom to do what I want. I'll try not to take up too much of your time, Mr. Heron. I know you're busy."

Maybe I just imagined a note of sarcasm, but I did up another button on my shirt and sat up a bit more professionally.

Beverly didn't seem to notice and continued. "I'm worried. Cass came back from the actor's workshop last night. He got the lead role in a new play at The Ajax, and went up to the workshop to practice. He was supposed to stay there all week, and then start rehearsals down here next Monday, but he's back already. He won't tell me why but it's plain to see that he is very upset. He can barely hold himself together." She hesitated while deciding how much she should tell me. "There was something that Cass said that worries me. It was that there might be a lot of money involved. Involved in what? I don't know. He wouldn't explain it. I don't remember ever seeing him this way and I'm afraid he might be in some kind of trouble. The reason I'm here is to say that if you know any way I can help, I want to do so. I still love Cass. He's a good man and I don't want to see him get hurt. Mr. Heron, if you know something, or if there's anything I can do . . . ."

"To be honest, I don't really think there is." I wanted to reassure her, but didn't have much to go on.

Beverly carefully uncrossed her legs, picked up her case and moved towards the door. I padded along behind, feeling about as competent as a bare-footed tap dancer.

"Thank you, Mr. Heron. Sorry to bother you." She was at the door, but was not leaving.

"Sure you wouldn't like a coffee. It'll only take a minute."

"Mr. Heron, there is something else. I don't know how to say this but someone, some people, feel very strongly about this merger, and, well, he, they have a history of getting what he wants."

Except for a son, I thought.

"And when there's that much money involved, bad things can happen," she said, as directly as she could manage.

Ms. Whitney was warning me, but her timing was a little off. I said, "I really haven't much to do with the merger, but I'll keep my eyes open."

"Please," she said impatiently. "The woman Cass is seeing is Judge Plumworth's daughter. I know that. He picks her up every time he drops me off to deliver documents, or whatever. I'm not blind. I don't expect him to wait. He's always gone by the time I finish meeting with the Judge, and I'm sure she's gone with him. I take a cab back to the office."

My two cases had overlapped—working for Fuller on the affair, and working for JJ as security for the Judge, and I suddenly realized why. The Judge must be the guy who was chosen to write the letter of approval, the LOV.

"Judge Plumworth is going to decide whether the merger goes through, isn't he?" I said, half as a question and half as though I knew it all along.

"Of course he is. The filing is due by the end of the day next Monday, and he's going to rule in favor. But it's pretty messy. I'm sure Father has put some pressure on him and I suspect that Governor Smithey has, too. Whitney and Whitney Investments is one of the Governor's biggest financial backers, and the Governor's got a campaign coming up. The Judge wants to sit on the State District Court, and that's in the Governor's hands. When the merger gets approved, Plumworth gets his appointment from the Governor, the Governor gets campaign funds from Whitney, over and under the table, and Whitney and Fuller get to combine and compete with the big boys. Everybody wins."

This group was wound together so tightly that if one strand broke the whole mess would fly apart like a house with a gas leak when a chain smoker drops by to follow up on an illicit affair with the bored housewife.

"And," she went on, "if the Judge finds out that Cass and Helen are, well, together, he has no choice but to recuse himself. He can't rule on a case when his daughter and the son of the applicant are in bed together, if you know what I mean." She ended angrily.

I knew she was warning me to watch out for her father. "You're telling me that someone, we won't say who, wants me off the case. At least through next Monday. And that I should watch my back. I appreciate that. Thank you."

"Goodbye, Mr. Heron." Beverly was out the door, her crisp self again, heading toward the stairs.

I followed her into the hall. "See you, Ms. Whitney," I called after her brightly. "And next time I'll try to be wearing shoes." An attempt at humor that I hoped she hadn't heard. I turned and walked back into my apartment, seeing it for the first time through Beverly Whitney's eyes.

14

MS. WHITNEY LEFT ME enough time to get dressed and drive to the Park to meet Doctor Dollar. I picked up a couple of sandwiches on the way. The traffic was light and I arrived at the park with a few minutes to kill, enough time for a quick stopover at the records office in the courthouse. Ms. Grange had been there since the beginning of time, a gray-haired grandmotherly woman with a steel-trap memory.

"Good morning, Mr. Heron. What are you looking for today?"

I gave her the name and approximate date for the Plumworth will and off she went. By the time she returned I was due for my appointment on the park bench.

"Sorry it took so long," Ms. Grange apologized.

I checked the signature page quickly and handed it back. It was the right will, signed and notarized. "I'll ask Kathy to take a look. She's a lot better at this stuff than I am."

"That's true," Ms. Grange said, a bit too readily.

The sky was dark. Low clouds hovered above and there was rain on the way. Fall was asserting itself and the park benches were empty. I settled into one to wait for my financial physician. The fat pigeon was still there. I dug into the lunch bag to see if I could cheer him up with a bit of bread.

Looking back toward the courthouse, I remembered Corbutt and Kathy strolling by. They didn't repeat the show today, but another familiar figure was hurrying along the sidewalk. I recognized the awkward stride. It was Sonny Plumworth, wearing a safari jacket and khakis, looking like he was going on an elephant hunt. He hurried up the courthouse steps and pushed through the revolving door. Henry Cadman came down the sidewalk from the other direction, crossed the street, greeted me with a nod, and plunked himself down on the bench. The wind was picking up and we were both wearing Burberry knock-offs, which gave our meeting a secret agent aura. Pass the stolen documents, please. I gave Cadman a veggie wrap instead, which he looked at suspiciously before biting off a tiny corner.

He frowned. "One hundred and twenty pages long, for Chrissake! And loaded with jargon. I did the best I could, and probably lost a couple of clients who got tired of waiting to give me their money. Why can't you be in the used car business or dentistry so I could get something out of this?"

"Don't give up hope. You may need me yet. Why, just the other day I heard that your wife was seen with . . . ."

"Shut up Johnny, before I hit you with this, this, whaddaya call it, veggie wrap. I said lunch, for Chrissake!"

"So tell me," I moved back to the subject, "what's holding up the approval? And by the way, I've learned that it's Judge Plumworth who is deciding."

"Right you are. Maybe you're not so bad at this detective thing. The Judge is going to decide on this approval, yes or no, and file the papers by this coming Monday, but somehow I wonder if he has even read the thing. In fact I wonder if Fuller has either. It's legal and all, but when you read the fine print it sure is one-sided. Whitney takes control. It's more of a takeover than a merger. Fuller must be panicked, thinks he could go under and is willing to take anything."

"I'm getting the impression—let's just say I've been told—that Whitney is prepared to get rough to push that merger through." I was visualizing the stack of hundreds that I walked away from. "What's in it for him?"

"Beats me. He'd be picking up a pretty weak outfit, but there must be something he's got his eye on."

"Now suppose," I kept going, "that the son of one of the merger guys and the daughter of the Judge are, shall we say, in bed together. That might throw a monkey wrench into the works, no?"

Doctor Dollar was dumbfounded. "You mean that's what you've been digging up? How come I have to read the financial stuff and you get to spy on people having sex?"

"Let's just say, suppose it's so," I hedged.

"Okay, suppose it's so. The Judge has to be an unbiased arbiter, and if he isn't, he obviously shouldn't be ruling on the deal. Somehow, the concept of fornication suggests a bias might creep in. If he's off the case, the whole process goes back to square one, could take months to get it through. I could see where neither Fuller nor Whitney would want that to happen."

"Some other stuff you might find interesting," I went on. "The Judge wants a promotion to the District Court, has worked for it all his life. The Governor is the guy who would make that appointment. The Governor could also, I assume, make sure that it was the Judge who got picked to look at the merger. Whitney is one of the Governor's biggest campaign contributors. Whitney wants the merger. The merger goes through. In theory everybody wins."

"You win too, Johnny. Now you've got me interested. Why is Whitney pulling so many strings to get this thing through? Maybe I can find a way to get into Whitney's portfolio. I have some friends who are pretty good at that stuff. If you want to stay in this private eye thing, you should bone up on your computer hacking skills."

"Doc, have you ever seen a baby pigeon?"

"What?" He kept munching on his sandwich.

"Seriously, no one's ever seen a baby pigeon. Do they just come out full grown?"

"Shit, Blue, what brings that up?"

"And when there's two, they're twins, right? Because they come out at the same time."

"Yeah. Fraternal twins I think." The Doctor reluctantly decided to go along for a bit.

"Suppose the pigeons, the babies, decide to get together. That's not legal, right?"

"That's incest, I guess," Doc said, "but I'm not too sure about pigeon law."

"Then who gets the nest egg?"

That stopped him. "Blue, would you like some of this bread, wrap, whatever you call it, to feed the pigeons?"

"No thanks, Doc. You'd probably better get back to work."

"Yes, nice talking with you, Blue, and thanks for the lunch. You know this veggie thing's not half bad," the Doctor added somewhat reluctantly. "Add some tuna and you might have something." He thought for a moment. "Blue, do you think a pigeon sandwich would taste any good?"

15

THURSDAY EVENING, I DUSTED off my best suit for the Judge's party. A dark conservative number that, to those in the trade, had private eye written all over it. The button-down collar and the cuffs were right out of the fifties, but I've heard that retro is in style. JJ said I had to do a little blending in. Just a job: hang around the edges, keep eyes and ears open, try to pick up anything out of the ordinary, as if a party featuring the Governor and a gaggle of his big donors had anything to do with ordinary. I wasn't really looking forward to the formal stuff, but I was thinking that I might run into Helen again. She had moved into a small room in the corner of my brain and kept inviting me to drop by.

The driveway was packed with cars, limos, and cops. Valets were shuttling the black Mercedes of the latecomers around back near the stables. I parked at the end of the driveway by the gatehouse, next to Helen's sparkling blue Lexus. Muscles Corbutt was checking people in. He knew me from way back, but he apparently felt the need to ask for my credentials and then spent some time looking them over and asking questions. Probably wanted to get revenge for a past insult that I had no doubt paid him, or more likely to let me know that he was flirting with Kathy. All in the line of duty. I thanked him and went inside.

The place was bustling, crowds of people I didn't know but would have read about in the Metro Section, if I read the Metro Section. They clearly didn't make the sports pages. The guests, about eighty-percent male, stood in small groups making small talk with one eye on Governor Smithey. He was in the center of the room, with Judge Plumworth at his side, meeting and greeting the sycophants.

A figure by the door caught my attention. He was a plant and he looked familiar. I think the giveaway was that he was acting like me, trying to look relaxed while covering the room with one eye. There would be an accomplice—it didn't take me long to spot him—on the far side of the room. Tweedle-dum and Tweedledee. I knew they weren't working for JJ. Maybe the Governor brought a couple of his thugs along to keep him company.

Whizzie was running around greeting people, checking on the hors d'ouvres and punch, and generally pretending to be important. I was most comfortable standing by the bar. The punch tasted like the caterers had emptied the dregs of the liquor cabinet into a bowl and added a few gallons of Kool Aid. I ordered a martini—Bombay Saffire and three drops of dry vermouth—mainly for the wide-brimmed glass and to feed my James Bond fantasy. Someone had to be brave enough to face the Governor, tell him to his face what others whisper behind his back. Someone had to take charge, to face the enemy, to take up the challenge. I knew that was me, no matter what the risk. I started across the room. The crowd parted before me like the Red Sea. Governor Smithey sensed trouble and looked at me over his shoulder. A hush fell over the room. I spoke first and my words brought a gasp from the crowd: "It's about time, Guv, I . . . ."

"What the fuck are you doing here?" The spell was broken by Douglas Whitney, standing at my elbow with a less-than-friendly stare.

"I happened to be in the neighborhood and saw a chance to get a free drink, thought I'd drop in."

"You don't seem to know what's good for you, do you?" Whitney said in a low voice. "Maybe you'd like to meet a couple of my friends."

I spotted Tweedledum moving towards us. I realized that he was the friendly chauffeur I'd met before, but his brass buttons had been replaced by a black-and-white pin-striped suit. Coming from the other side of the room was Tweedledee. His ears were focused on me like a tiger's ready to pounce on his prey, and now I could see his round head, the same no-necked round head that was driving the green SUV that was following Castor. I stepped closer to Whitney, looked down at him, smiled, and said, "Just what do you think your friends are going to do to me in the middle of this party?"

"Why, Mr. Whitney. How nice to see you." Whizzie had appeared. She seemed to materialize wherever in the room she was needed, without actually walking through the crowd to get there. "Come, the Judge would like to say hello." She took him by the arm and off they went.

Tweedledum retreated back to the entrance, and Tweedledee to the opposite wall. I thought it would be a good idea to make some new friends and blend in a bit. I tried and failed to start a conversation with a couple of lawyers, and I did equally badly with the financial types; but I managed to waste some time with a young aide of the Governor who was trying to figure out who I represented and why I was there. Small talk wasn't my specialty, so before long I found myself standing again by the bar, filling up on peanuts and another martini, and watching the crowd.

◆   ◆   ◆

Guests were still drifting in and I was surprised to see Beverly and Castor among them. Fuller must have sent her along to keep his fingers in the wallets of the rich. With his merger in the Judge's hands, he probably felt that it wouldn't look right for him to be brown-nosing around the premises, a thought that didn't seem to bother Whitney Senior. I figured Castor was brought along as arm candy. This was setting the stage for some awkward moments, if not fireworks, and one of those potentials was walking in the door at that moment.

Mr. Potato Head, aka Sonny Plumworth, had just arrived, still wearing the safari outfit. He headed straight for Castor. Out of the corner of my eye I saw Whizzie take off on the hypotenuse to try to intercept him. Sonny, red-faced and pissed off, apparently his normal state, got there first. He hissed a curse at Castor that I couldn't hear—but I figured it was something like "you cocksucking whore of a slime bucket!" My curses are usually more colorful than those that come naturally to pissed-off people. Whizzie stepped in front of Sonny, and Beverly tugged at Castor. It was like watching two parents pull their squabbling toddlers apart at the playground. They were pretending for the crowd that the whole thing was just a joke, but the steam was visibly rising from Sonny's blond buzz-cut. "I have to change, a tie or something," I heard him mutter, and as an afterthought, "you money-grubbing imposter!" Off he went like a teenager sent to his room.

Castor pulled a pack of cigarettes from his jacket and was about to light one when Beverly pointed him toward the side door. Smoking outside was the rule. I watched him leave to the darkness of the garden. Tweedledee started edging towards the door, and I pushed and shoved my way through the crowd, taking a few under-the-breath insults, and one helpful, "The bathroom is the other way."

Stepping into the night it took a few seconds before my eyes adjusted to the dark and I could pick up the glow of Castor's cigarette. He stood about fifty feet away, gazing into the night. Tweedledee was in front of me, slowly moving toward him, his hand stuffed into his jacket pocket. The yard on this side of the Mansion was deserted, leaving just the three of us to play out the scene. I stepped behind No-Neck, stuck my pen into his kidney, and whispered, "Don't make a move, or it will be the last move you make, the move, that is." Damn, that shouldn't have been so hard to get right!

He froze. He was familiar with deadly threats and knew when to follow orders. I reached around and pulled a nasty-looking Beretta from his jacket. Then I replaced the pen with the Beretta.

"Walk. And don't make a sound." I didn't want Castor to spot us. I pushed No-Neck to the side of the building, keeping the pistol hidden between us.

"You didn't have a gun, did you?" he growled.

"I do now. Thanks. Even has a silencer. You weren't planning to use it, I suppose?"

"Shit!" He stiffened.

"Don't do it! I suspect you might need this kidney." I pushed the metal into him.

We edged around the corner of the turret to the front lawn moving like a wounded four-legged insect. Muscles and two other officers from the precinct were stationed there.

"Corbutt, I've got a perp for you."

"I didn't do nothing," were No-Neck's first words.

"Could you get this guy in cuffs, and take him in? Concealed weapon. Just get him out of here."

"You can't. I have a permit," No-Neck protested.

"Never saw it," I said.

"What d'ya know," Corbutt grinned. "Looks like you found some garbage." He was apparently familiar with the thug, and seemed downright pleased with the idea of tossing him in the lockup for the night. "That's a nice present you've brought me, Blue, and that's a nice piece you're sportin'. Beretta 84 Cheetah, I believe. A bit small, but packs a powerful punch—didn't know you had one of them."

No-Neck made a grunting sound.

"Actually," I corrected Corbutt, "I carry a Precise V-5."

"A what?"

"A Pilot Precise V-5, rolling ball, extra fine point, black ink, good for figure drawing, keeping a diary, and stopping thugs from doing something stupid."

"You bastards, I'll sue!" No-Neck growled.

"Sure," Corbutt said, "and the court gets a chance to dig through your record. That should be rich." Corbutt tightened the cuffs and gave the officers instructions.

"Fuck you all!" No-Neck made sure he got in the last word as he was led away.

Corbutt pushed No-Neck to the police cruiser, opened the rear door, and shoved him in. The policeman's attempt to push the perp's head down was unsuccessful, but No-Neck didn't seem to feel the thud his head made when it bounced off the metal door frame.

I watched the patrol car turn down the drive, the blinking red lights reflecting off the low-hung branches of Pine Tree Lane. Castor should appreciate having No-Neck out of the way. Maybe he could get me a couple of free tickets to his next play.

16

THE GOVERNOR'S RECEPTION CONTINUED in high gear.
The guests were shaking hands, chatting, laughing, and positioning themselves in the hierarchy. The bartender had
guarded my martini and I returned to my spot by the bar.
The booze had increased the noise level and encouraged a
few rowdies who were beginning to make the Governor's en-
tourage nervous.

Fireworks potential number two appeared at the door:
Helen had turned up wearing a long red silk number that
stopped about half way up her breasts, leaving two thin
strands to cover the rest of her shoulders. A pair of long ruby
earrings dangled down toward the straps. More make-up
than usual, but not enough to cover dark circles under her
eyes. The vision had been crying. Something had happened
up the coast that was pushing her toward the brink. I stayed
on the edges and watched. Castor had returned and he so-
cialized and watched Helen. Helen chatted with admirers and
kept one eye on Castor. When young Whitney abandoned
Cass and headed over to greet the Judge, Act III began. Castor and Helen, as though being drawn by the same magnet,
moved toward the terrace door and slipped out, one after an-

other. I started elbowing my way through the crowd—this time trying to keep the elbowing at a minimum. It took me awhile to get across the room. I moved to the glass door and stood to the side, enough to take advantage of a clear view to the outside. The terrace was lit by long streams of light shining through the French windows, and it looked like the stage of a theatre in the round. Helen and Castor, the star players, were not happy. In fact they looked totally distraught. It wasn't exactly a fight, but the tension was about to pop the straps on her gown, a thought that quickly grew in my imagination.

I would have stayed out of this scene, but Beverly was approaching the terrace doors. I knew it would be better to be the first to interrupt.

Helen looked at me, and tried to regain her composure. "Well, hello again." A pause, then, "Have you met Mr. Fuller, Detective . . . ."

"Heron," I helped out. "Johnny Heron."

"Hi." Castor held out his hand. "Nice to meet you. You look familiar, have we met before?"

"Likewise." I took the hand. I was beginning to feel that I'd known the guy for a long time.

"Maybe I'd better go," Helen said.

"No, please don't," Castor pleaded.

Over Castor's shoulder I could see Beverly coming through the door. Helen also saw her, and quickly moved toward the unlit lawn, making a hasty retreat before she was face to face with her lover's fiancé. Then she turned back, looked around, and then at me, and she said seductively, over her shoulder strap, "I'm going to my house. This gown is too tight." It was an invitation that I was not about to pass up.

She disappeared into the dark as Beverly took Castor's arm and asked, "Where is she going?"

"Oh, the Judge's daughter?" And Castor searched for words. "She lives there, I think."

"I'm Johnny Heron," I stepped in. "I think we've met."

"No, I don't think so," Beverly answered abruptly, taking hold of Castor and leading him back to the party.

I turned and headed across the dark lawn to the gate-house.

17

I CROSSED THE GARDEN, lit by the full moon, a white colorless light laying shadows. I instinctively followed a path of least visibility close to the thick hedge, as though my visit was one to be watched, registered by some big brother. I knocked on the door to the gatehouse, lightly, and hearing a faint sound I thought to be an invitation, I pushed the door open. The room was dark. A shaft of moonlight coming through the door lit a shape in the center. A white pedestal of flesh, it seemed, with a rounded divided top. She was there, but her back was toward me, legs straight as marble columns and folded at the waist so her hands touched the floor. She was completely naked. The cleft puffed between her legs with vertical lips, mustached on both sides, and crowned with the dark depression centering her bottom, like the bowl that holds the holy water at the door of a cathedral. She was motionless, facing the floor, waiting for me. She knew that I would come.

I closed the door, pushed off my pants, underwear and socks with one motion, and stepped close to her, taking each cheek into hand and gently spreading. I think my cock must have jumped like a released jack-in-the-box. It played against her and picked up the juices that were flowing as from an underground spring. I tried to slide inside her slowly, resisting the urge to plunge, and she said nothing, spoke not a word, but held her hands to the floor to keep balance. Sliding in and out, a rhythm I played against by moving my thumb back and forth along the crevice of her ass in counterpoint. In her position I felt that my cum might drain down through her, lodging in unnamed cavities that would empty as she unbent and turned toward me. I saw her face and she stiffened. She froze as she looked seemingly through me to the garden outside. Finding courage, or perhaps despair, she then pushed me to the floor, on my back, and settled her buttocks over my face. She began to rock, moving her love button back and forth across my nose as though rubbing a sock on a washboard. Her juices and my cum poured out as a rich soup that I devoured. She bent forward. I think my cock was in her mouth, but the feelings were all over me now. I was unsure what was where. Her thighs clenched, and clenched again, leaving me without air, although by now I had little interest in breathing. I was submerged in the deep. She relaxed, then turned and lowered herself upon me, her breasts touched me first. She lay against me, from head to toe like the statues of Shiva and Shakti welded together. The docent at the museum said it was not erotic, that it was the merging of her rationality with his emotion. Perhaps that explained why I never took religion seriously.

Helen began to lick my face, like a smooth-tongued kitten, and I slid again inside her, quietly, as though returning home. We kissed, so briefly, but it seemed too intimate. She rested her head beside me, cheek to cheek. She, looking down, and I looking up at the shaft of moonlight that lay across our bodies. I remembered seeing the moon setting over Vesuvius, casting sparkles across its slope, sparkles that turned out to be the reflections of broken glass scattered by tourists. It made me chuckle, and she chuckled too, and then again, until I realized she was crying, sobbing softly into my cheek. I tried to enclose her, gently stroking her hair, hugging her to me. I no longer knew where one of us began and the other ended. We lay, me inside her, she holding on tightly as though to keep from plunging into some dark abyss.

18

HELEN HADN'T MOVED WHEN I disentangled our bodies. She lay as if asleep. I dressed in the dark, and opened the door. A shaft of moonlight shone through the door and fell across her. I stepped out, closing the door softly. The Mansion glowed ahead, but the lawn was dark, the hedges throwing shadows, and the moonlight helpless against the strong Mansion lights. I walked back toward the entrance quickly, thinking it was late and I'd better get back to the party before JJ decided to take me off the payroll.

Halfway up the lawn, just as I stepped from behind the hedge, my foot hit something with a thud. It felt like a bag of unmixed cement. A car swung around the circular drive. Its lights swept over me, and the body.

"Shit!" was all I could come up with. I knew at once who it was, and I knelt beside him. Castor was still warm. I checked his pulse—there wasn't the slightest trace of life. Another car swung around. This one stopped, the headlights upon us. The body lay in the middle of a circle of scraped earth and uprooted grass, which spoke frighteningly of Castor's last minutes. I saw the gleam of broken glass scattered on the lawn and picked up a shard. The smell of the kerosene-like punch was strong, but there was something else there also. I couldn't place it. As I stood up, my eye caught a figure at the door of the gatehouse I had just left. Helen stood frozen for a moment, staring at the dead form, then vanished inside.

Someone in the car screamed, and figures began running towards the scene. I singled out Officer Corbutt, and called him over. He followed my orders somewhat reluctantly, but he could see I wasn't about to tolerate any objection. "Just keep everyone back." I pointed out the broken glass. "And don't let anyone touch those until forensics gets to it. I'll get JJ."

That wasn't necessary. A suit and tie appeared with JJ inside. He quickly took charge, ordering officers to cordon off the scene, pushing away the suits and gowns that were gathering. "It's okay. We've got a sick guy here. Everything will be fine. Please, go back inside. Help is on the way."

Something told me that Castor didn't just decide to die there without some help, and I'd been in this business long enough to know that when a murder occurs it's not a bad idea to find the last person the victim fought with. I spotted Whizzie running toward us. "Where's Sonny? Do you know where's Sonny is?" I demanded.

"He went to change, to his room, but that was a while ago." She pointed toward the Mansion and I took off for the side door that opened into Sonny's rooms. It was unlocked. Clothes were scattered about, including the khakis and that ridiculous coat. The closet door was open. I guessed Sonny had found an appropriate suit, dressed in a hurry, and rushed back to the party.

Leaving the room as it was, I went back around to the terrace and slipped into the living room through the French doors. The merriment was continuing unabated, the guests oblivious to any disaster. JJ had already returned to the party and was talking privately with the Judge, telling him, no doubt, that everything was under control, that some guy had a heart attack or something and the police were taking care of it. The Governor continued shaking hands like an automated doll. Nothing was going to get between him and his fundraising, filling the coffers for the upcoming election. I caught JJ's eye and nodded toward Sonny. He was by the gun rack with a group that looked like his golf buddies. We both moved toward him from different directions. Sonny was involved in a tale of hunting heroics that revolved around his being face to face with some large beast. He was about to slay the dragon when JJ said in his best cop manner, "Could I talk with you for a moment, Mr. Plumworth? Privately. Let's step into the Judge's office." I thought Sonny was going to unleash his usual string of curses, but he apparently recognized that he was looking at the law, and he dutifully followed JJ into the office, leaving his buddies to finish the story for him. I stayed in the background. If Sonny saw me he would fly off the handle and JJ wouldn't get anything out of him.

Rumors from outside were beginning to float around the room and dampen the good spirits. The crowd started thinning, but those who had drunk most of the punch bowl were slow to register the exodus. The Governor knew exactly how to exit, making it look as though he had something more important to attend to. Nodding left and right to the guests, he left with a coterie of bodyguards and sycophants. I followed them out. In front, the valets were working hard for their tips, and cars and limos were filling up and moving down the

lane. Whitney's Mercedes moved past. Tweedledum had returned to his role as Brass Buttons and was driving, but the
tinted windows assured anonymity for the passengers. The
departing guests followed in a train of limousines moving
slowly around the circle and down the drive, taking part in a
funeral procession they were unaware of. There was no longer
an exposed corpse to show up in the headlights, the coronary
crew had done its work and Castor had been moved away.
Yellow tape encircled the crime scene, but the reason behind
it wasn't apparent. Each limo carried away a different version
to tell of the evening's events.

I moved to the edge of the tape and looked for a familiar face. I spotted a forensic guy I knew and drew him aside.
"What's the thought? Heart attack? Seizure? What?" I asked.

"We think his heart stopped, maybe a coronary. But poisoning is certainly a real possibility. We're checking the glass,
could be arsenic, maybe strychnine."

I thanked him, and contemplated the sad picture before
me. Beverly Whitney was standing in the shadows at the edge
of the lawn. Irene Wiseman was beside her, holding her hand.
Tragedy casts pettiness aside, and can be the glue to form un-
likely alliances.

I moved around the opposite side of the circle of tape,
toward the gatehouse. My heart was working its way up my
throat as I walked back across the lawn, along the hedge, and
to the door where I had last seen Helen. There was a light
inside. I knocked gently, and opened the door for the second
time that evening. Not much had changed, but the room was
deathly quiet. The moon, higher now, illuminated only the
door sill. It would not have cast a light on our bodies now,

but it did when we were lying together. The significance of that suddenly struck me. The moonlight fell across us only because someone had opened the door. It was agonizingly clear. Castor had come, opened the door, seen us, and left. *It was Castor Helen wanted to see.* Castor, whom she wanted to seduce back into her arms, to put back together what they had lost. She was asking *him* to come to her, not me. "You arrogant ass!" I condemned myself. She had looked at me when Beverly appeared because she couldn't directly invite Castor in front of his fiancé. They had fought and Helen didn't think she could get him back but was desperately trying. I shivered, just as she had shivered when she realized that the wrong man was inside her. And then she gave in. She must have thought Cass wouldn't come, would never come back to her, and so she gave in to me. But he did come. He found her in another man's arms and left thinking Helen was lost to him. Maybe he was waiting, maybe walking back when his heart stopped. He died on the lawn outside, or was killed. When Helen heard the commotion, she came to the door, and she saw the body of the man she loved, of the man she had wanted to make love to. She must have known then that he had come for her, and that he had left broken-hearted.

I called out for Helen, softly, but there was only silence. The bedroom door was open, and my nerves were getting to me as I looked in. No one was there, but the back door was open. Next to my car was an empty space where Helen's Lexus should have been. I guessed she would return to the last place that they were together, in love together, before something destroyed everything. It would take hours to get back up the coast. I hoped I would get there in time.

19

AT THREE IN THE morning the oldies were holding their own against God, but I wasn't in the mood to sing. I kept punching the FM buttons on the car radio until the speakers reluctantly admitted the sonorous tones of a classical music announcer. He was introducing a string quartet whose name could only be pronounced by a fluent German speaker. Or was it Hungarian, or Budapestian? Those smooth talkers just made up those accents, I thought, a jealousy that came from forgetting my two years of high school French. In my apartment when I couldn't sleep, I would search nighttime radio for a loud rock group with an electric guitar and a relentless drummer, noisy enough to drown out the metaphysical shudders. Tonight, on the road, chasing Helen to the north, the emptiness was deep enough to ask for company and Bela Bartok fit the bill with a string quartet that skirted around normalcy. I was comforted by sounds that spoke of spaces yet unexplored, for the usual closets of my mind were filled with old clothes that I couldn't find the nerve to throw away.

The strip malls struggled to brighten the mood. Closed but glowing with wasted electricity to advertise their existence. Cathedrals for the rituals of purchase that allow us to find meaning in things, in products. The small towns that break the strip are dark and deserted. Tonight, I can't picture people sleeping in these houses. Rather they appear as empty shells, where once upon a time humans lived. The rare car that passes is surely party to some illicit activity: a theft; a wanted criminal escaping; a lonely private eye who's running from the nagging idea that he is part of a Shakespearean tragedy, those plays I hate where the main character is headed over a cliff from the start and every scene pushes him relentlessly to the unavoidable in Act V.

The sun was only thinking about rising when I drove through New Troy again. The small New England town was stretching and yawning, preparing for another day that would be like yesterday, or tomorrow. An early riser had turned on a couple of lights in the home of the burger and fries, and I wondered if it was the kid who had given me directions. I remembered them and made my way toward 7 Sunset Lane. Morning hadn't officially arrived and the dirt road to the cliffs was still in the province of night creatures.

A possum lay by the side of the road. Road kill, I thought. In the rear-view mirror I watched him get up and trundle off. Another bend and I faced a doe with two fawns. The deer gracefully bounded into the adjacent field, stopped, turned, and looked at me with wide eyes as I drove by. An active imagination has its disadvantages, for the deer weren't nearly as afraid as I was.

One more turn and I could see the peak of the cottage roof lit by the first ray of the morning sun. Helen's car was in the drive, and I was relieved to have guessed correctly. I again parked next to the lonely blue Lexus.

Three steps up to the porch, the screen door squeaked, the porch floorboards groaned, the swing hung motionless, and the cottage door was open. There was no answer to my call. I went inside and was faced with emptiness, a few pieces of leftover furniture and a bucket to catch a drip from a leaky ceiling. I could see a glimpse of a bed in the back room. There was no warmth to the place, as if it had been abandoned after last year's tourist season. Next to the only couch was a table sporting a 1978 *National Geographic*, last week's *Seaside Times*, a pair of familiar ruby earrings, and a photograph. On the couch and the floor beside it was the red gown, matching red panties, and a pair of high-heeled shoes. Helen was not in them, and nowhere to be seen.

It didn't take me long to chart her path and I bolted through the door and up the slope to the granite cliffs. She was standing, far ahead, perched at the edge. Facing the sea like the gulls who always face the wind to assure a quick take-off and escape. Even from this distance I could see her hair blowing straight back, flashing the golden rays of the rising sun. Her naked body glistened alabaster white. A figurehead on the prow of a magnificent ship, steering it toward disaster.

My cries were blown back to me by the wind. I began to run up the hill but was slowed by lead legs, lead feet, lead shoes. She may have looked toward me before she sailed, or maybe I just wanted her to. With arms raised she tilted forward, pivoting over the edge in slow motion. Two full turns, then brought to a halt by the rocks below. A sound that I could not hear, but would never forget.

◆　◆　◆

A couple of fishermen were running toward the broken body on the rocky shore and I knew the local constabulary would appear soon. Helen's death would provide them with stories to tell for years to come. I had no intention of starring in those tales, and I ran for the house. I raced through the room, slowing only to pick up the photograph and grab the panties from the arm of the couch. Maybe the police wouldn't notice, and hopefully she had worn them long enough to leave me a scent I could hold on to.

I made it back to town by the time the flashing and wailing squad car rushed by. I didn't want to be remembered on a wanted poster, so with my usual clear thinking I screwed up my face to look like a monkey as they passed. It was an act that effectively covered any real emotion with deep embarrassment. I don't remember much of the drive back, only that the sun shone with a cold, cold morning light.

20

I TRIED TO SMILE at Kathy as I entered the precinct office, but she wasn't in the mood to deal with an unshaven deadbeat. Wearing slacks—must not have expected me today—she looked over the top of her coffee mug and pointed the way through the office door.

"We're holding Sonny on a murder charge," JJ explained, without waiting for me to ask. "Looks like Castor was poisoned—fox glove, we think, but the final analysis will come from the lab in a day or two. We dug through the call history on his cell phone. That morning he got a call from Castor Fuller. Don't know what they talked about, but it looks like they must have fought for some reason, judging by Sonny's reaction when he saw Castor at the party. It's not much of a case, all we have is some pretty circumstantial stuff and we're not even sure when he got dressed and returned to the party. He's bringing in some pretty high-priced legal defense. I suspect he'll be out by this afternoon."

JJ continued, "As for Whitney's bodyguard, or whatever he is, he had a permit for the gun and didn't actually do anything, so we had to let him go. If he was going to shoot young Fuller, he obviously got the order from Whitney. So we don't know why Sonny might want to kill Castor, and we don't know why Whitney wanted him dead, too." JJ stopped long enough to look up at me.

"She's gone," I blurted out. JJ stiffened. He wasn't used to seeing me about to decompose.

"Sit down, Blue. Have a coffee. I can wait." He buzzed Kathy to say, "No interruptions. Nobody!"

We sat and listened to the noise from the street, the voices from the outer office. Twice I tried to start. On the third try it worked, and I went through the story in reverse. First, she jumped, then I ran after her, then I entered the cottage, then I drove up the coast. I didn't go back far enough to get to the rendezvous at the gatehouse, but I have a feeling that JJ filled that in for himself. Who knows, or wants to know, what fantasy a bald Chief Inspector would have created.

"Something's missing here," JJ said quietly, drumming his fingers on the side of his desk.

"Try this," I said, and handed him the photograph that I took from the cottage.

"The guy looks familiar."

"I agree, how about a younger version of Fuller. George Fuller, the father of Castor, with a pretty young woman holding what looks like a very young baby. He's the guy who hired me to find out about this affair, and he wanted me to find out about the place they stayed. Then he called me off the whole case—said to forget the whole thing."

We both fell silent again trying to build a story that would fit.

The intercom buzzed. JJ answered impatiently. "Well?"

Kathy's voice came over the speaker: "Thought I should tell you, Chief. A report from up the coast just came in. Suicide. Judge's daughter."

"I know," growled JJ, and pushed the off button.

"That means the Judge will know. We'd better do some interviewing."

"Me? Wouldn't that be like the witness cross-examining the prosecutor?"

JJ ignored me. "You've just been hired again. My personal assistant."

"Can we wait 'til tomorrow?" I asked.

"Sure." JJ pressed ahead. "But you've got to talk to Fuller first thing in the morning. Then come by here and we'll go to the Mansion. We'll talk to the Judge, and Irene Wiseman, I suppose." I think JJ knew that the best therapy would be to get me back on the job.

"Okay," I agreed. "Pretending to be a cop again will no doubt be good for the soul." I was supposed to get up and leave, but I sat. JJ waited until I had morphed back into a third-rate private eye imposter.

"Mind if I ask Kathy to do a little research. I think a trip to Records is in order, and maybe Probate. Should check on a will and maybe some marriage details."

"Okay," JJ said. "But quit stringing her along."

"What. You think I still have half a chance?"

"Chance! You know you knock 'em dead with that smile of yours. Everything's great until the good-for-nothing side rears its ugly head."

"Right, JJ. And why don't you quit working twenty-four hour days and go home to that beautiful family of yours?" I nodded toward the photo on the desk.

"Yeah," JJ sighed. "Trouble is I think they prefer it when I work late."

"Give me a break! Your problem is that you just can't imagine anyone putting up with you. You've got a perfect family. Just get out of here and be a dad for a change."

"Okay, but don't go messing with Kathy's head again. She has enough on her mind without trying to figure out what to do with a deadbeat like you."

"Thanks, JJ."

"Yeah. Sure."

I stood up, smiled at JJ and left for the outer office.

I stopped at Kathy's desk to ask if she could follow a couple of leads in the County's files. Her response was cool and efficient. "I'll start with Fuller, see what I can find. Then there's the Judge too, Plumworth."

"Yes, please, if you could"

"Please?" She looked puzzled. "Are you all right?"

"I think so." I lied.

"Okay, that 'please' goes a long way. I'll let you know."

Leaving the office, tired, shaken, heading home to get a bit of sleep, realizing I still loved Kathy. Deadbeat—hmm, maybe it's a bit too accurate.

21

Since Fuller had thrown me off the case on Tuesday, I had pushed the details of his office into my brain's cold storage. Saturday morning, I'm dusting them off. I dropped in without calling ahead. Marie was just walking out the door and was surprised to see me. "Mr. Heron," she blurted out before catching herself, "I thought you were . . . ." She stopped, probably remembering that much of what she knew about my work was gained by listening through the office door.

"Surprise, I'm back. I have to talk to Fuller. Maybe you'd better check your files again while I'm in there."

Marie didn't see the humor. "I'm off for the day. Go on in."

George Fuller sat behind his desk, motionless, staring into space. He looked at me with sad disappointment. I suppose he had hoped that Cass would walk in.

"Mr. Fuller, I'm sorry. I know it's hard. He seemed a fine boy." I consoled him, hoping he wouldn't take my visit too badly.

"What do you want?" He scowled. "I thought we were through—you're off the case! Don't bother me!"

"Trouble is, Mr. Fuller, there's a murder investigation under way. The cops, they'll be all over this thing. And I'm afraid that as soon as they find out that you hired me to check up on Castor, they're going to get interested in you."

"Interested in what? I didn't do anything. I've lost my boy." He stifled a sob.

"It would be best," I continued as gently as possible, "to let him rest peacefully, I agree. But you know the law. Someone has to pay."

"That Sonny guy did it, didn't he?"

Loud footsteps, a crash, and the door flew open. Beverly Whitney burst into the room. "You did it," she screamed at a stunned Fuller. "You had him followed and they killed him. Poisoned him. Why? What for?" She broke into tears, waving her hands helplessly, desperately trying to make some sense of it all.

"Bev, I didn't. I was trying to help. Trying to . . . ." He trailed off, not wanting to tell her that Castor was having a fling. Her fiancé was dead, and he thought she didn't know about the affair. Why make it worse?

He got up and went to her. She shook and cried and he wrapped his arms about her, trying to protect, trying to do the impossible. He took her gently into the waiting room and came back in a few minutes.

"Let's make it quick," he asked me. "What do you need to know?"

"The last few days, just this week, Castor went up the coast with Helen and stayed in a cottage. You know the address. What else do you know?"

"Yes, yes I do," Fuller began. "It's her place. Or rather it was her place. Castor's mother, Leda, she owned the cottage.

Yes, it was probably the smallest thing she owned. You know, Castor was born out of wedlock, as they say. Leda and I, yes, we had a brief fling. Very brief, actually. It was a one-nighter. We didn't know each other, met at a bar. She was married to some hot-shot. But she wanted the baby. She went up to the cottage for the last months of the pregnancy, when it began to show. I went up as much as I could, on week-ends mostly. I couldn't get away much. Everything had to be kept, ah, yes, quiet." He dropped in and out of his 'ah, yes' stutter mode. He would never make a good liar.

"Her husband knew?" I asked.

"Yes, I think he did. I never met him, didn't even know who he was. Leda didn't want me to know, and I didn't really want to know. Somehow he, ah, allowed her to have the baby, as long as it was hidden. And Leda had a boy. Castor was born, yes, with a midwife, right in that cottage."

I waited. He was going to continue, and I was getting more interested all the time.

"We made up a lie. She told her husband the baby died. Died at birth. She decided to go back to the life she had. It was painful, as you might imagine, but for her own reasons she left Castor with me and went back. I think she couldn't imagine a life without the glamour, or whatever it was she had." Fuller dug in a drawer for some Kleenex, couldn't come up with any and settled for his sleeve instead. "She helped me with some money, and I took Castor and left. Went back to Iowa—that's where I grew up. Went back home to my parents. I wanted to get Castor out of here and give him a good life, so I raised him there with grandparents to help."

"What happened to Leda?" I wanted to keep him going.

"I never saw her again. I don't know what happened. I didn't want to know, either. It was a one-night stand and, yes, that was that. I felt blessed to end up with the boy, ah, the sweet boy. But now he's gone. Oh God. What'll I do? Oh God." He was close to breaking down.

"But why did you throw me off the case?" I pressed on, knowing it was harsh but figuring better me than the police. Maybe I could head them off if I could get a few answers.

George Fuller waited a while before answering that. Then with a sigh, he confessed. "Look, you know the market lately. The mortgage crisis and all. Well, my business has been taking a hit. A bigger hit than my investors realize. My only chance is Bev's father. The Whitney of the big financial outfit. I'm sure you've heard of them. They might buy into a merger, and I have enough clients to keep them interested. But it had to happen soon, and, let's face it, if my son is cheating on their daughter that just wasn't going to play. I hired you to see if that was true, but I didn't know what I planned to do next. I thought maybe if I knew more I could work around it and smooth things over, or at least keep them under cover."

There was more to this than I figured, but that was usually the case.

"The Whitneys have money, and they make money. I wasn't doing well. And Castor wanted to be an actor. He wasn't any good at making money, that's for sure. I wanted to make sure he had, get him a bit of, ah, a nest egg."

Fuller stopped, then added threateningly, "And if you go spouting off about the affair, or my finances, or whatever, it isn't going to play either." He hesitated again, trying to pull himself together. "But what does that matter now, anyway. What does anything matter? Oh God, I don't know what happens now."

I couldn't help. I told Fuller I would try to keep things quiet. I was pretty sure that a Fuller-Whitney merger wasn't responsible for Castor's death. I thanked him, but he didn't seem to hear. I left, and found a shattered Bev sitting in a reception room chair.

"He wasn't trying to hurt anyone, Ms. Whitney, really. He was just trying to make sure Castor could hold up his side when you got married."

"It was my fault," she suddenly blurted out. "I shouldn't have done it. Why didn't I just stay out of it, but I didn't want my father to bring George down." She held her head in her hands and sobbed.

I put my hand on her shoulder and held it there until the shaking calmed. "You're not to blame," I tried to reassure her. "Please, go in and see Fuller. He needs you now—why don't you go in."

I left them, an unhappy pair, but at least a pair. What was Beverly trying to tell me? She didn't want to let him bring George down, and what did she have to do with Castor's death? It made no sense, except that people who are close to tragedy often feel responsible. I never did like tragedy. So why was I a private eye, someone who makes a living, sort of, off shattered lives?

22

THE OUTER OFFICE WAS empty, but I could see Kathy sitting at JJ's desk. She looked up as I entered, and actually seemed happy to see me. "Good morning, Mr. Blue." She smiled. She was dressed casually, in week-end garb. A loose silk blouse, unbuttoned over an elastic halter top that didn't try too hard to cover things up.

"You're working week-ends again," I said. "You need a home life." I dropped into the chair facing JJ's desk. I'd been here enough recently to feel at home again, and I sat back, nonchalantly crossing my legs. I was trying not to be too obvious in my fascination with the bumps that Kathy's nipples had formed through the stretched material.

"Look who's talking," Kathy replied. "Sorry you had to get up so early on Saturday, hangover recovery day, but I need to be filled in a bit. You saw Fuller this morning. Did you learn anything that could help me while going through the records?"

"He's pretty upset, as you might imagine. Losing one's only child has got to be one of the worst blows you can suffer. There's no mother around. She disappeared early on and he raised Castor himself. Now he loses him. It's lousy!" I was trying my best to allow Kathy's breasts to keep my mind off Fuller's sorrow. I've always thought that the best way to deal with metaphysical shudders was to cover them with pornographic fantasies. I was only partly successful. "And Beverly Whitney was there. She knew Castor was having an affair, but I think she still loved him. It wasn't a happy scene."

Kathy was quiet, and concentrating. I could see that her brain had gone into high gear, although that wasn't the part of her on my mind.

"There's something else though. Something is troubling Ms. Whitney," I continued. "She feels responsible for the whole mess. I can't see how or why."

"Maybe she called for the LOV." Kathy was in sleuthing mode now. "Somebody had to get Justice interested; it's too small a case for them to pick up without cause. She knows the ins and outs of both companies. It could be she knows something."

"Yes, but," I objected, "Fuller would have been really pissed at that, and so would her father."

"Exactly. That's why she did it anonymously. She knows something about Whitney's firm and doesn't want the merger to go through.

"Kathy, you're brilliant . . . and you have the most beautiful breasts."

She stopped, held her hand motionless in the air for a moment, and then with one smooth motion she drew her fingers under the left strap, dropping it over the shoulder under the loose sleeve. With a second casual gesture, she pulled the elastic neck line down, revealing the left one of the most beautiful breasts. The pose reminded me of Renaissance paintings where a diaphanous gown had often fallen off the shoulder of a beauty, and almost always it was the left breast that was bared. I was working on a 'the left is evil' explanation when the phone rang, and without missing a beat Kathy answered in the most professional manner. "JJ Cake's office, Inspector McGregor speaking."

I was sure that her nipple was growing toward me, and I studied it closely to see if that were so. I read once, no doubt in a bad detective story, that mother's milk tasted like the juice from a coconut.

"Oh hi, JJ. Yes, he's here. I'll tell him." Kathy calmly spoke into the phone, as if nothing was out of the ordinary.

We sat silently, Kathy looking directly at me, and my gaze alternating between her brown eyes and her left breast. Someone came into the outer office, and the door to JJ's office began to open. With a fluid motion Kathy swept the elastic top back into place, covering her breast but leaving the strap off to the side. She flipped her shoulder so that the blouse covered up the still errant strap. Muscles Corbutt poked his head in. Seems Corbutt always found a way to show up when I was with Kathy. "Hi, Kathy. Oh, hi, Blue. I'm just looking for JJ."

"He's not here now—he's on his way to the Plumworth Mansion," Kathy replied, unruffled. Corbutt left, and Kathy got up. "Best be getting back to work," she said as she walked by me.

I reached out and held her thigh to stop her, then touching the side of her cheek guided her face down to mine. It was just a short, very gentle kiss, followed by an embarrassed nose rub. But we both knew that was too playful for the moment.

She bent back toward me, and this time she let her tongue glide slowly over my lips. She stood up and pulled the strap back into place. Professionalism took over again. "JJ is on his way to the Mansion, wants you to meet him there. I'm headed for Records. I might have something for you later."

"Something?" I wondered.

23

LATE AFTERNOON, THE LIGHT was beginning to fade when I drew up to the Mansion gate. Officer Corbutt, who seemed to turn up everywhere, was the ID cop and waved me through. Even he could see that it wasn't the right time to play games with my credentials. I slowed down as I passed the gatehouse. It was dark and closed up, and the flowers seemed to have wilted on their stems. I parked behind JJ's shiny blue-and-white Chief Inspector squad car.

Higgins answered the ring. He looked at me suspiciously, as though I was responsible for this whole mess. I found JJ in the living room. Last time I was here this room was alive with brand-name suits and expensive gowns, jammed to the brim with the glitterati. The limo-set, each trying to buy another rung up the ladder, that endless ladder with no top, only a greater distance to fall. Now the room was empty enough to hear JJ's greeting echo off the walls. JJ managed to stay chipper throughout rapes, murders, and general mayhem, which is why he could stay in the force while I bailed out.

Whizzie came out of the Judge's chamber, trying to keep her composure and do the secretarial thing. That was pretty gutsy considering her bed partner was under investigation

for poisoning his sister's lover. "The Judge will see you now."
It was a weak excuse for normalcy.

Judge Plumworth was behind the desk, his face the color
of a blank sheet of paper. I guess when you're on a murder investigation it stands to reason that you see ghosts. Few are
left unaffected by death, and if you've just lost your daughter, and your son is under suspicion, one could be expected
to look a bit peaked. He was a Judge, though, and he knew
the ritual and was prepared to answer questions.

JJ started right in, asking if the Judge knew Castor.

"I saw him for the first time at the party. Never met him
or heard anything about him before that. I don't know who
he is, or was."

"We've checked Castor Fuller's mobile," JJ pressed on.
"Wednesday evening he called here, your office."

The Judge looked surprised. "No, I never got a call. I told
you, I never saw hide nor hair of the kid. Tough luck, gets
himself killed on my front lawn. And then poor Helen. I
don't understand." The Judge thought a bit. "I don't suppose
he's related to the Fuller of Fuller Investments?"

"Actually, he's George Fuller's son," JJ explained, watching to see the Judge's reaction. The Judge looked puzzled. He
was trying to make some sense of the Fuller connection, but
he didn't volunteer any thoughts about the merger, or his role
in approving it.

That line of questioning was going nowhere, so JJ moved
on. "Why would Sonny be cursing at him?"

"I have no idea," the Judge replied, "unless Sonny was
upset over the affair with Helen. I don't know." The Judge

shifted in his chair and opened a random file from a pile on his desk. JJ ignored the hint to end the interview.

"And Sonny and Helen, some issue over money?"

"Yes, that's true. They're twins, you know. Their mother died in the hospital when they were born. She was quite well off, well, actually all that you see is, was, hers. This Mansion, everything. It all went to the kids, but Sonny was left in charge. The will gave him the power to make all the decisions about who gets what. That didn't sit too well with Helen because he isn't very generous," explained the Judge, bravely trying to hold himself together every time Helen's name came up.

JJ pressed on, gathering lots of irrelevant details about the twins, the party guest list, who made the punch, and where the valets came from. The Judge answered as well as he could, but said that we'd have to check with his secretary about the details of the party arrangements. JJ switched to asking questions about the Governor and which donors were present, but the Judge decided he'd spent enough time with us.

"If you don't mind, I don't think I can deal with any more questions today, and it seems like you've covered most of the important areas. If you want me to help in the future, I'll be glad to oblige," the Judge said with an air of finality.

"That's fine," said JJ. "Thank you, sir. I know it's a difficult time and you've been very patient with us. I'll let you know if we come up with anything."

"What about Sonny?" the Judge asked. "Is he still your chief suspect?"

"For the moment, yes," JJ answered. Then hoping to make the Judge feel better he added, "To tell you the truth, there isn't much solid evidence."

We were done, and left the Judge with our sympathies and apologies. "Whizzie next," JJ said. "Have to go through the party details. I think she'll talk to me, but you'd better wait here. She thinks you've got something to do with all this."

I settled myself back into the deep couch in the empty living room and stared at the fireplace. One of those fake log things that light up and flicker when the switch is thrown, and doesn't warm anything. My mind wandered. It was stuck on the strange will. Something Castor said in the phone call must have thrown Sonny over the edge. I found my attention had moved up to the painting over the mantelpiece, the family portrait of times gone by. The young Judge, and . . . . For a moment I refused to believe what I was seeing. The face in the portrait. I remembered the photo I had taken from the cottage, dug into my pocket and pulled it out. The panties came too. I carefully folded them and put them back—I was glad they didn't appear when I showed the picture to JJ. The woman in the photo, the mother of Castor, had a one-night affair with George Fuller. Castor was the result. The woman in the painting was the wife, now deceased, of Judge Plumworth, mother of the twins Sonny and Helen. The photo and the painting showed an identical face. The pictures were of the same person. Leda was the mother of Castor. Leda was also the mother of Sonny and Helen. My God! Castor and Helen were brother and sister!

24

BEETHOVEN'S FIFTH BEGAN PLAYING from my breast pocket. It was Kathy.

"Hi there, Sky Blue, how's life?" she teased.

"Okay, lover girl, but it's just Blue."

"I spent some time down at the courthouse, and I think you might be interested."

"The coffee shop, in an hour," I said.

"See you there, Blue-berry." She was incurable.

It was Sunday morning. I needed some coffee, and sharing it with Kathy was just what the doctor ordered. I'd spent most of the night lying awake with the two pictures of Leda rolling over in my mind like a pair of blue jeans in a dryer. The photograph was in the cottage, probably left there by Leda. Helen ran across it, or Castor showed it to her. They were in love, they were rolling about in a bed, and they discovered they were brother and sister. I worked through a number of possibilities. Maybe they fought, maybe they tried to make love, maybe they blamed each other. In any case, they left the cottage early and came back, and their world was shattered.

By the time I pulled into the lot behind the diner, the only thing I was sure of was that the photograph had thrown the love affair into a shambles. When Helen saw Castor at the party, she was desperately trying to salvage something, knowing all the while that it was hopeless.

The One-O-Clock Diner was where Kathy and I met when we didn't want the entire precinct to eavesdrop. We took a booth in the corner, and the waitress knew to bring us an order and then leave us alone.

"So the Court has some good info; what have you got, or did you call me here to make a pass?" I started.

"Blue, will you get your mind off sex, or are you walking a tightrope where that's all there is to hold you up?"

"Kathy, give me credit. You know 90% of everything in the world is about sex, like it or not, and . . . ."

"And?"

"And 90% of sex is about everything else."

"Hmm, so the one track has a philosophical rail. When we have some time you'll have to explain that, or better yet, demonstrate it."

"I think you just called my bluff, Kathy. But I could take a stab at it, take the plunge, dive right in . . . ."

"First, the will," she interrupted, taking on a business-like manner. "The wife's will. Her name was Leda, by the way, Leda Bertrand Plumworth. It's pretty much as we've heard. She willed the Mansion and the money to Sonny."

"To the eldest," I added. "It still doesn't add up."

"Well, the actual wording is that control goes to the first-born, and since everyone seems to agree that Sonny was born first, he got it. Bad luck for Helen, missed it by a minute or two."

This was sinking in slowly. "The first-born! That's why everybody seems to want Castor dead!"

"What, tell me?" Kathy demanded.

"It doesn't say Sonny; it says *first-born*. Right?" I asked.

"First-born. You want to see it, I have a copy," she answered testily.

"You know what that means?" My voice was getting louder. "It goes to Castor! Castor gets everything! Holy fuck!"

"What are you talking about? And whatever it is you'd best calm down or it will be in tomorrow's paper." Kathy was getting exasperated.

"Kathy, this is getting dicier by the minute. Leda, the mother, had an affair a couple of years before the twins were born. She had a kid!"

For once Kathy was speechless, she just looked at me with a "well, go on" expression.

"Leda went up to a summer vacation house—not much more than a two-room shack up the coast. It's where Helen jumped." I tried to explain, but was just confusing the issue.

"You're not making much sense," Kathy noted dryly.

"She, Leda, that is, went up there and had the baby. Out of sight, no scandal, no gossip. Kathy, there's an old portrait in the Judge's Mansion of him and his wife. There's a photo that I picked up at the cottage up the coast of Fuller and his one-night stand and their baby. Those two women—they are the same person!"

"Wait!" Kathy interrupted. "You're saying that Castor and Helen had the same mother—that they were brother and sister? Or, more exactly, *half*-brother and sister?"

"Exactly. That baby was Castor Fuller." I tried to stay calm. "Castor Fuller, the first-born child. Castor Fuller, the guy who stands to inherit everything. Castor Fuller, the guy everyone wants to bump off."

"Why doesn't everybody know this?"

"Leda was married to the Judge and had an affair with George Fuller. It was just a one-night stand. So she tells her husband—we know now that's the Judge—that it was a difficult birth and the baby died. Then she gave it up. Yes, gave up the baby to George and returned to her grand life. Cut all the strings and sent him out west to raise the kid. He had no idea who she was, or who she was married to, or where she went. Still doesn't, I think. He just took the kid, went back to Iowa to his parents' place, and raised the boy with their help." I felt like I was making this up as I went along.

"I think I'm getting the picture." Kathy began to work this out. " Leda must have felt awful about leaving the child. She made a decision she felt she had to make but just felt terrible about it. Who wouldn't? So when she wrote her will she was making up for it, in a roundabout way."

"You know, she died in childbirth when the twins were born." I followed Kathy's lead. "She wasn't even thinking about the twins when she made the will—they weren't in the picture. Probably wrote the will a year earlier. Used 'first born'—that's clever."

Kathy continued. "Do you think she thought someone would turn up Castor if she died? Or maybe it was just a way to ease her conscience, as best she could."

"I took a quick look at the will the other day. Guess who's the notary? Whitney, himself."

"So," Kathy thought for a moment. "There's a pretty good chance that Whitney knew about Castor from the beginning, but never said anything about it."

"Yes. Because he was so close to the estate, he sees money and doesn't want to go out and search for a lost heir and give it all away, so when Leda dies in childbirth he just keeps quiet."

"And when Castor shows up, Whitney sees trouble and puts his thug on Castor's tail."

◆　◆　◆

The waitress came by, refilled the coffees, and left us again. I think she was getting curious, as we were looking pretty intense. Kathy didn't tend toward the melodramatic, but I could see her eyes mist up. "They were lovers. Brother and sister, and lovers. Once they saw that photo at the cottage, they realized they were doomed. There's no room in this world for a brother and a sister, even a half-brother and a half-sister, to be lovers, even though it seems quite reasonable that they would find a magical attraction. It was a love that couldn't be duplicated, but that had no possible future."

"Not to mention that it's against the law," I added.

We sat speechless until the silence made me too nervous. I tried to get back to detective work. "I wonder if Sonny knew how that will was really worded. He was a baby when she died. He wouldn't have read the will."

"Listen to this!" Kathy pulled herself together. "You know when you look up these documents, you have to sign in."

"Yes." I could see that Kathy had more on this.

"So just last Wednesday, guess who signed in to look at the will." She waited, letting the tension build for the punch line. "Castor Fuller," Kathy said triumphantly.

I let this sink in for a moment. "Castor, when he found out that he was related to the Plumworths, gets curious about the will and wonders if he would have anything coming to him. He looks up the document and it says he is the heir, the prime first-born heir. The phone records show that Castor called Sonny Wednesday evening. Castor calls Sonny, raises the issue of inheritance. Sonny realizes that Castor is going to horn in on the rights to the estate. Now we've got a motive for Sonny."

"You can probably guess who signed in to see the will on Thursday morning," Kathy said.

"Sonny. I saw him go into the courthouse, Thursday around 12:30."

"Right."

"So by the time the party rolls around, Sonny has figured out that he will lose control of the Mansion, the money, everything, if Castor remains on the scene. We've got a murderer staring us in the face. We've got two murderers staring us in the face, Sonny Plumworth and Douglas Whitney. Kathy, hold on to this for a bit, would you? I want to see if I can get Whitney to admit to knowing about Castor."

"How can you do that?" Kathy asked.

"I have my ways," I said with as much macho as I could muster.

Kathy gave me one of her 'get real' looks. "Well, good luck, Mr. Bond."

We stood up to leave, dropping a generous tip on the table to thank our waitress for the privacy. At the door Kathy, with her flair for the dramatic, said, "Oh, by the way, Blue Bell, I found something else you might be interested in.

Everything's alphabetical over there, and I came across this." She handed me a couple of Xeroxed pages, and left for her office. Didn't she ever take a day off?

I glanced at the papers, then looked up to watch her walk away. My mind would have been working on a fantasy involving her swaying buttocks, but her latest discovery had caused my computer to crash.

25

AFTER LEAVING KATHY, I walked back to the park. I could see Whitney's long black liquor-cabinet-on-wheels parked beside his building. There was a good chance he would be at his desk, and on Sunday the office staff wouldn't be hanging around to mess things up. I was working on a plan, and had refined it as far as getting to the front door . . . by the time I got to the front door.

The door opened just as I approached, and two suit-and-tied Ivy-leaguers walked out. Overtimers—I hoped they were the only ones. They were headed straight for Leroy's Bar and didn't even notice me. I caught the door before it closed.

I entered into a two-story-high hall, centering on a large sign-in desk that was deserted. The lobby was designed to intimidate visitors—a large high space wall-papered like a Versailles throne room. A staircase up the side led to a balcony where I could see a frosted glass door inscribed with Whitney and Whitney in letters large enough to read from the suburbs. A huge crystal chandelier highlighted the room. On the walls hung a veritable sausage-fest of political portraits. Over the desk was the largest: Governor Smithey looking as though he'd just signed the Declaration of Independence. He was surrounded by Judge Plumworth, a couple of senators who looked familiar, and a few genuine signers. George Washington himself hung over the stairs, staring down at the large body who had materialized below him. Tweedledum, fully brass-buttoned, had arrived to guard the staircase. I started walking toward him.

"We're closed! Come back tomorrow."

"I'm going upstairs," I announced with as much authority as I could muster.

"No you're not!"

"Try and stop me," I challenged.

So he did. He pulled a pistol from his uniform—they must have gotten a two-for-one deal on the Berettas—turned me around and stuck the barrel in my ribs. "Okay. Now you're going upstairs, but we're doing it my way. The boss might like to give you a little talking to."

We started up the stairs to Whitney's office. I was wishing he was using a fountain pen instead of the lethal piece of iron that prodded me. I really didn't like this gun-in-the-back thing. I still wasn't sure what my plan was, but I knew that it required that I enter Whitney's office completely in charge.

I stepped on to the balcony. "Spider! It's a spider!" I shouted. "Look here!" I batted at a crawling thing on my shirt.

"What?"

"They're poisonous—look at him! Christ! Get him off of me!" I started slapping at the critter.

"You wimp! Shut up!"

"Ahh, he's in my shirt!" I yelled. I grabbed the front of my shirt with my right hand, and began jumping up and down and ripping off buttons.

Tweedledum was getting pissed off. "Will you cut that the fuck out, you . . . ."

I grabbed off another button with my right hand, and at the same time swung my left hand down on the pistol. There was a sharp crack, shattered glass, and the frosted pane that used to say Whitney and Whitney, now just said Whitney. I spun around, grabbed the barrel of the gun, and forced it down. Tweedledum was one step from the top, holding on to the pistol for balance. I put one finger of my right hand on his chest and pushed. He teetered for a moment, staring straight at me with a puzzled expression, then let go of the Beretta to grab hold of the banister for support. He was tilted backwards at 45 degrees when the wood gave way. The weight was too much for the old wood, and the banister snapped. The crash that followed was impressive—250 pounds of thug bouncing down the stairs to end in a large lump at the bottom.

I was about to run down the stairs when I saw that Kathy had come in and was watching the melodrama. The compost heap at the bottom of the stairs began to shake and stir. It seemed to re-enact a couple of billion years of evolution, squirming from primordial ooze to reptilian creature, and finally rising to its feet as an ape. Never did make the last step. Kathy pulled a revolver from somewhere—how did she carry that without my spotting an extra bulge?—and used the threat of a bullet to the head to convince Tweedledum to revert to a sitting position. He slumped down on the bottom step, emitting a series of simian grunts. Kathy gave me a look that said, 'I don't know what the hell you're doing, but I've got this one covered so go ahead.'

I turned back toward Whitney's shattered door. Through the hole in the glass I could see Whitney's face—white as the whipped cream on a lemon meringue pie. The door opened easily, sliding broken glass across the floor. I led with the pistol. Whitney was sitting at his desk in the middle of his idea of the Oval Office. A standing American flag was on one side, and some other flag on the other. On the desk a small American flag, a brass eagle, and a bronze toy cannon added to the ruse. I remembered Fuller's desk and decided that it must be bad for business if the boss has any papers on his desk. I suppose the idea is that he is so good that he doesn't actually have to do anything to make stacks of money. Whitney was shrinking behind the desk, visibly trembling, not used to looking into the wrong end of a gun.

I cut the greetings short. "Your man's a lousy shot. Believe me, I'm a lot better."

"I'll call the cops . . . ."

I ignored him, and waved the gun around. "Let's start with why you wanted young Fuller dead."

"Not me. You've got nothing! Put that gun down!"

"What gun?"

"There was no way my man could have poisoned him," Whitney pleaded. "You sent him to the clink. Remember?"

I pointed my finger at him, except that my finger was a gun. "Last Wednesday—you got yourself a sweet piece of the action. A big chunk if you could break the will for Helen Plumworth. A mondo commission—like huge!"

Whitney was facing a man with a ripped open shirt, waving a gun around like a lunatic, and it was clearly getting to him. His large noggin was bouncing around like a bubblehead toy on the dashboard of a dune buggy. He began to stutter, "But, but I, but . . . ."

I raised my voice. "And if Castor turns up—no job, no commission, right?"

"What are you talking about?—and don't point that . . . ."

"You wrote the will!" Whitney was pale and silent. "You wrote it for Leda. You put that first-born crap in there."

"Yes, I wrote it," Whitney admitted. "But Leda wanted . . . ."

"You wrote first-born instead of Sonny Plumworth, didn't you?"

Whitney took the bait. "You dimwit! *Castor*, not Sonny. You're not even in the ballpark. You're playing with half a deck. What do you want anyway? We could make a deal . . . ."

"What do I want?" I lowered the gun and my voice: "I just got what I wanted."

I decided to keep the gun and stuffed it into my pocket, thinking I'd actually rather take the toy brass cannon. Whitney was sputtering about police and lawsuits when I slammed the door. The other "Whitney" fell out and shattered on the floor.

◆　◆　◆

Kathy was sitting comfortably in the receptionist's chair, her pistol resting in her lap. Tweedledum was still sitting on the step, with a storm cloud on his face and a large bump on his head. He was framed by a couple of pieces of shattered banister and a few brass buttons on the floor.

I told him he could get up and get going. "You're needed upstairs. The boss wants to give you a raise." I looked at Kathy. "Shall we go?" I held the door for her and tried unsuccessfully to catch sight of where she hid the gun.

"So," Kathy said as we walked back across the park. "What was all that about?"

"I talked Whitney into admitting that he knew who Castor was. He did; he knew it all along."

"Nice. You've got a motive, but do you have any idea how he might have done it?" Kathy asked.

"Details, details. That's for you police officers to figure out. And thanks for stopping by, Inspector McGregor. A nice surprise."

"I saw you headed for Whitney's—didn't take a genius to see that you were going to need some help. But what if Whitney cries foul and gets us involved?"

"Imagine the reputation of a lawyer who writes a will, then covers up the fact that the wrong guy is getting the estate, and then tries to get a piece of it for himself. No, as long as we can't pin the murder on him, he'll keep quiet."

"What happened to your shirt?" Kathy asked.

"It was a spider," I explained.

26

I WASN'T SURE HOW the Judge would take the brother-sister thing, but he should be told. It would all come out in the next few days anyway, so why not try to break it to him gently, although almost anyone else familiar with this case would do a better job than I would at breaking the news gently.

I didn't want to explain to the Judge that it was stylish now to wear a shirt without buttons, and as the drive from the town center to Pine Tree Heights took me past the Main Street Mall, I made a quick stop at a will-sell-everything outlet store that stayed open on Sunday. The result left me looking like I was selling rides at an amusement park, but what the hell, the Judge was going to need cheering up.

I was turning into the now-familiar circular drive of the Mansion when a pick-up truck passed me on the way out. A very familiar, rusty, mud-covered pick-up truck that made me remember a leg full of thorns. I drove around the circle without stopping and started after the red rear lights. This time I was the tail as the truck headed for the town road.

The traffic was light enough to allow a good distance between us. I did a lot better at impersonating a real TV cop this time—no garbage trucks, but I did have to run a couple of red lights to keep up. The Toyota was headed to the south end—immigrant land, an old single-tract development on the city's edge. A bit run down since the cement plant opened up and the suburban types moved out. Each of the wooden houses was now home for two or three families who came from south of the border in search of the good life. All the surrounding communities bitched, but they were selfish enough to realize that if they cracked down they would be cutting their own grass and mopping their own floors. It was beginning to dawn on me who drove the Toyota, but the why was still avoiding me. Finally Higgins pulled up to a small wood-frame house with a nicely tended yard and walked around back. He wasn't suspicious, never looked back, just climbed the so-called fire stairs to the upstairs rooms. I followed suit—parked in front and walked around to the back and up the stairs. A light came from the kitchen window next to the landing and I could see a woman was busy at an old two-burner bottled gas stove. She looked very familiar. What the hell was she doing at Higgins' house. I felt like I was taking jigsaw pieces from a fish picture and a cat picture, and trying to force them together to make the Taj Mahal.

The knock startled her. She didn't answer but ran to fetch Higgins, who opened the door a crack.

"Hi Champ," I grinned, and pushed my way in.

Higgins blanched, and didn't try to hold the door. I walked into an apartment that seemed three-quarter size. The ceiling was low and tipped towards the walls, a couple of small rooms carved out of what once was an attic. Higgins and Marie Henry stood frozen in place. The last time I saw her was in the reception area of Fuller's office, and before that, pulling papers out of a filing cabinet very close to the inner office door.

"Good evening Ms. Henry and . . . ," I said. "I must say, I didn't expect to find the two of you here."

Higgins was no hardened criminal. He fell into confession mode before I could even ask the questions. "I'm sorry, sir. I didn't mean anything, *nada*. I was just sposed to scare you. I don't, I mean *No say* . . . I'm not . . . ." He fell into a mixture of Spanish and English that really didn't need translating.

"How about you invite me in, offer me a cup of tea, or better yet a shot of tequila, and then we can have a heart to heart," I said with as little threat as I could muster. "And do tell me what names I should be using."

I pulled a chair from the kitchen table and sat down. I learned that it was Mr. Pete Hernandez and Mrs. Maria Hernandez who sat opposite me, side by side on a flowery couch that fit nicely with my new shirt. It was as though I was a long-lost cousin stopping by to catch up on marriages, births, deaths, and why the hell was Higgins trying to run me over and what was Fuller's secretary doing here?

Higgins started again, but his wife interrupted with no trace of an accent. "Look, Mister Heron, it's not Pete's fault, really. He's a good man. It's me, I . . . ." She stopped, looking like a trapped mouse, and obviously didn't want to continue.

"Mrs. Hernandez, you may as well tell me." Again I tried to sound sympathetic, but us private dicks make a practice out of sounding threatening, and this wasn't coming easily. "You can tell me or you can tell the police, and I think that telling me could be a lot less painful." Well, I tried, but I guess the threat thing just works better.

"*Por favor*, we don't want trouble," Mr. Hernandez started. "We do our jobs."

"You work for Fuller?" I said.

"Well, yes. You know it's easier to get a job as a receptionist if your name is Marie Henry instead of Maria Hernandez. We need the money, Mr. Heron. We have to send some home, my mother." She fought back a tear.

"So you need a bit more, something on the side?"

Mrs. Hernandez was having trouble continuing. Higgins put his arm around her and took up the slack. "I get a salary from the Judge and Maria works for Fuller. It would be . . . I mean, enough, but there's people at home."

"Yes," I said a bit impatiently. "And who gives you the bit on the side?"

"Whitney," they said in unison, and then looked at each other.

"Mr. Whitney," explained Maria. "He wanted to know a bit more about Fuller's business so he pays me to give him some information now and then. He wants to merge with Fuller anyway, so what's the harm?" She said the last sentence without much conviction.

"And Fuller wants the merger too, so it would seem they are both on the same side anyway," I added.

"Yes, so everybody wins."

"Mrs. Hernandez," I interrupted. "Any time you hear about a deal where everybody wins, you can be sure it's a con game. You're telling me how badly Whitney wants a merger, which financially should be of very little interest to him. A money-loser for a guy who everyone seems to agree is Mr. Hard-Ass Money Maker personified. I think you know why.

I want to know, and the cops are going to want to know, so I think you'd better get it off your chest."

"Whitney and Whitney is about to crash!" she blurted out.

Maria looked as though she expected a spanking, but I didn't understand. "Go on," I said. "Explain."

"Whitney's about to go down the drain. He's hanging by a thread." As Maria spoke I realized she was a lot brighter than my prejudiced mind had figured her for. "He wants to merge with Fuller. Somehow he thinks that can save him."

"Maybe so," I said, "but it doesn't get very close to explaining why Higgins, I mean Pete here, tried to Toyota my ass to the pavement."

"I wasn't going to hit you, *creame!*" cut in Pete. "I was just supposed to scare you, confuse you. *Eso es todo,* buy a day or two. Keep you away 'til the Judge ruled. *Eso es todo lo que habia.*"

"You know what he was going to say?"

"Judge Plumworth has decided to allow the merger." Maria took over. "That's the gossip in Fuller's office, and Pete's kept his ears open enough to back it up. Whitney senior has sweet-talked him, and the Governor has applied pressure too. The Judge has no idea of the trouble that Whitney and Whitney is in. The decision will be issued by the end of the day tomorrow. Whitney's just buying time until that paper is filed."

Maria added, "And he was afraid you'd reveal the Castor-Helen affair, which would force the Judge to excuse himself from the decision."

"How did he know about that?" I was learning a good deal about this case.

"Pete's not blind. Every time Castor would bring Beverly Whitney by and drop her off with papers about the case, Helen would sneak out and drive off with him. Actually I think that Castor first met Helen when he brought Ms. Whitney by a couple of months ago."

I didn't know for sure that Beverly had alerted the powers-that-be about problems with the merger, but it seemed pretty likely. If she did raise the red flag, it had inadvertently led to her husband's and Helen's first meeting. No wonder Beverly felt so miserable about her role. Pete had been keeping his eyes open, and now I thought of the figure hiding behind the hedge spying on me while I was hiding behind the gatepost spying on Cass who was in his car waiting for Helen. It was Pete Hernandez, the butler. He'd already figured out that Cass, the young Whitney's fiancé, was seeing Helen. He told Maria. Maria told Whitney Senior who immediately saw that this was enough to toss the Judge off the case if it came out. He wanted that positive ruling, and he wanted it fast, before he went under. A new Judge on the case would add a long delay, and the new guy might not be as susceptible to the pressure, might do his research a bit better and rule against the merger. It's hard to agree to a merger of two companies when both are about to go bankrupt.

"So did Whitney tell you to bump me off?" I figured to try and get it out in the open while tongues were loose.

"No, no! It was just to scare you, get you off the case for bit. Throw in a—how do you say—a monkey wrench." Pete was getting afraid now.

"A Toyota is a pretty big monkey wrench, don't you think?" I growled, remembering the briars.

"Not me. Really. I mean it wasn't sposed to be me. He was paying his *guardaespaldas*—how do you say—thugs, to do it but the guy followed Castor up the coast. I thought I'd fill in—get some dollars. I need some. You see Maria's mother's sick . . . ."

"No sob stories, okay?"

"I was just trying to follow you, from way back. You see me and I get afraid. But you came toward me. I thought you'd know me so I turned on the lights . . . just swerved at you. *Eso es todo.* To keep you from seeing me, that's all." The whole plot seemed stupid enough to be believed, but I felt like I should thank Pete. If No-Neck had been on the job, a coroner would have carried me out of those briars.

◆　◆　◆

It was Sunday evening and the Judge's ruling was due out by the end of the day Monday. The Hernandez involvement was messy but I was ready to drop it. I knew that I had to see the Judge before he officially filed that ruling. I'd get to the courthouse first thing in the morning and try to talk him out of it.

I had left the couple with, "Just keep your mouths shut for a couple of days. If you're lucky this might blow over." I was about to give a moral lecture on the evils of taking money on the side, when I thought better. My business didn't give me much of a pulpit to preach from.

27

THE TRIP HOME TOOK me back through the center of town. On a hunch, I drove a few blocks out of my way to pass through the Central Square, and down Main. The town was quiet. On Sunday night this community went to bed early, tired from a day shuttling the kids to church and play dates, and worrying about the approaching week of dead-end jobs. One light burned on the fourth floor of the professional building. I parked in front, found the lobby door unlocked and the elevator still on the fritz. Three flights and I was at the door of Fuller's office. The front room was deserted, but Fuller was in the inner office digging through the file drawers. He froze when he realized he wasn't alone, but upon seeing me, he changed his expression to resignation.

"You again. What the hell are you doing here at this hour? You got your money, right?"

"Sorry to be a bother. I know it's late, and you probably have to get up tomorrow."

"I suppose so. But I'm going to make the best of it. Tomorrow Castor was going to start rehearsing, down at The Ajax."

"Yes. I watched his audition."

"You did?" Fuller brightened a bit.

"I'm no critic, but he was good. Very good. A lot better than the other guys I saw."

"He loved that silly little theatre," Fuller said quietly. "I'm going to make it better. Get some money into it, maybe rename it."

"You don't think *The Ajax* sounds good enough?"

Fuller actually smiled. A sad smile, but a smile. "No, but *The Castor* doesn't sound much better."

"Mr. Fuller, I came here to tell you something. Can you take a minute?"

Fuller sat down wearily at the desk. "Sure. I've got all the time in the world."

"The merger with Whitney. You wanted it?"

"Yes, business is bad, but I want to get back on track now. I want to get some money into Castor's theater."

"Whitney's a crook. Don't you know that?"

"I know he's not too savory, but business is business."

"And he's about to go bankrupt."

The thought flowed over Fuller like a fine rain, softening the edges. I think it was something he expected, something he knew deep down but refused to see, a nasty truth that loses its power once it is acknowledged.

"He wants to merge," I continued. "Leave you with the bad debts and cut himself free. Can he do that?"

"Yes, I suppose, with the way it's written he could," Fuller admitted. "I was in a panic when I agreed to the terms. It looked like my only chance to survive." He put out his hands palms up. "What can I do? It's signed and sealed. I've done it."

Fuller wasn't stuttering. Grief seemed to have won over nervousness, and pushed out the ahs and yesses.

"I'm not a financial whiz, but let me try. You go to Whitney's clients, and you tell them he's about to go bankrupt. Talk to Henry Cadman if you need more info—you know him. I'm willing to bet that they'll come running to you like bees to honey."

"That's good, but there's a big 'but.' I signed it, and the Judge is about to give it the final approval if he hasn't done it already."

"Let me take care of that. Trust me, Mr. Fuller, that isn't going to happen."

I was more confident than I had reason to be.

"But . . . well . . . maybe I," was all that Fuller could come up with.

"Think of the theatre, *The Castor* Theatre."

"*The Castor*? No, the name doesn't work. I'm sorry." Fuller spoke half to me and half to someone who wasn't in the room.

"How about *The Swan*?" I suggested.

"*The Swan*. Why?"

"For Leda, for Helen, and mostly for Castor."

"*The Swan*. Oh that's nice. I can hang a big picture of Cass in the lobby." A tear started down his cheek. He didn't bother to wipe it off but stood up and went to the file cabinet. "I have the names of Whitney's investors somewhere here." He pulled out a drawer and began to rifle through the papers. "*The Swan*—Castor would like that."

I slipped out and took the stairs down. I sat in the old Honda for a bit. A slow rain had begun to soak the leaves on the ground and the night had settled in. I knew the rules: don't drive when there's booze in your gut; don't drive when there's a tear in your eye.

28

A CUP OF HOT water, two spoonfuls of instant, one more of sugar, and a package of non-dairy creamer and I was ready to start another Monday. I called Cadman before he left for work—he was just out of the shower and not pleased. "Good grief, Johnny, can't you at least wait 'til I have breakfast?"

"Sorry Doc, but it'll just take a minute."

"Make it quick."

"Remember Douglas Whitney? You were going to look into his finances."

"Yes, I did, and it's a muddy picture, but I think he's borrowed a chunk of money and put it into some pretty shaky derivatives. They're hard to pin down. You never know what they include, but there's one big one in particular, which may be headed south."

"My sources tell me you're right." I liked sounding important. "Tell me, if Whitney merges with Fuller Investments, or as you described it, takes over Fuller Investments, how can that help him?"

"I can see you'd like the worst-case scenario," Cadman replied. "Yes, under the terms of the merger, Whitney gets control. He could drop the bad loans on Fuller, and cut him loose. There's nothing Fuller could do about it."

"Thanks, Doc. Just wanted to be sure. Enjoy your breakfast."

The coffee would have tasted better if I had some milk, but the bottle in the fridge was as sour as my mood. Whitney's obsession with the merger made sense as he wanted to dump his debt on Fuller, although he still doesn't know that it was his daughter who threw the monkey wrench in the works by starting the approval process. He got around that by using his influence with the Governor to get the Judge to write it. The Judge depends on the Governor for his promotion and wouldn't want to screw that up by sinking the Governor's biggest donor, so he was about to write an approval. Whitney has everything back on schedule until I come along with the potential to expose a scandal that would sidetrack the process. Whitney makes a couple of attempts to get rid of me—first a bribe attempt, then a hit-and-run. Then he sends No-Neck to get rid of the nuisance, namely Castor. No-Neck tries at the parking lot but the weed dealer was there. He tries to follow Castor up the coast but loses him. Then Whitney sends Tweedledee to take a shot at Castor at the Judge's party, but I took him out of the picture. I should finish my coffee and drive downtown to see if it was possible to get the Judge to see the light.

◆　◆　◆

The county courthouse was one of the few buildings left in the town center that spoke of history, the years when we built columned replicas in miniature of the Parthenon in the centers of all our American towns. The square park remained, but the buildings around it had been mostly demolished for some new economic promise. The old hotel, a white wooden decorated wonder, had been replaced with an eight-story office building, a brick cube designed to house the professional offices that hung around the municipal center—the lawyers, bail bondsmen, and a liquor store all on the ground floor. It centered on a couple of big glass doors, and over them a sculptured frieze with angels or grapes or something that served as its one nod to decoration. The other two sides of the square had been blown away to allow two more lanes of traffic to get in and out of town as quickly as possible. Whitney's townhouse was left as a lonely relic standing on the corner. On the next block sat some one-story dime stores, or dollar stores, or whatever currency was considered cheapest at the moment.

The courthouse had always been a challenging building to breach. The security guards, posing as the nation's number-one defense system against foreign enemies, wave detection wands over your body while pretending it doesn't matter if you're male or female. The metal detectors, which operate intermittently, are run by a uniformed crew who rely on the scare in order to keep from going back to cleaning toilets. Next there is the bureaucracy, the sign-in: name, company affiliation, destination, and time. The Judge had a third line of defense in his outer office: another sign-in, reason for visit, with whom do you have an appointment, and please wait over there where the seats are filled with eager legal assistants with briefcases on their laps looking like they are waiting to see the dentist. I figured the Judge would wave aside the drill if I could just get to him, so I walked past the receptionist and barged into the office, quickly closing the door behind me to slow down the cop. He was so anxious to get his weapon out of the holster, he walked straight into the closed door. The

Judge looked up from his legal brief, or whatever it is that judges read—maybe the latest Grisham—saw me and realized that something was up that he couldn't ignore. He waved off the approaching SWAT team, threw a legal aide out of the office, and said, "Okay, Heron, this had better be good."

"Sorry, Judge, but I think I'm working against time. Your writ, decree, tort or whatever it's called: the Fuller-Whitney merger. There's some background dollars and cents that I think you should know."

"Thanks anyway," the Judge said quietly. "I filed it first thing this morning. It's done now, at least until the eager beaver ambulance chasers find a way to challenge it. But that takes months, so I'm finished with that for now."

I slumped down into the chair in front of the Judge's room-sized desk. I don't know why, but I felt responsible for what would become Fuller's further demise. On the other hand, maybe the Judge would get his promotion, and none of it should really matter that much to me anyway.

"Anything else?" the Judge asked patiently.

"Just curious, you honor," I tried to sound respectful. "Will you be sitting in the District Court this time next month?"

The Judge laughed without humor. "Are you kidding? Mr. Heron, I just ruled that the governor's biggest donor couldn't merge with a patsy firm and save his honor and career, and you think I'm getting a promotion for that. I don't know how you private eyes think the world works, but you don't have to be a genius to see that I'm going nowhere."

"You ruled against it?"

"Yes. All the pressure that was coming down from the Governor and Whitney and whoever got me curious. And then with Helen gone," the Judge choked a bit on that, "and Sonny up on a murder charge, the District Court looked pretty meaningless. I spent the last couple of days going through the data, and I realized that I was being played for a fool. My own fault, I suppose—I really didn't want to look too closely. Whitney and Whitney is headed for Bankruptcy Court. It's just a question of time—and not much time at that. That all has to be in the public eye before any merger can even be considered. The odd thing is that if Whitney collapses, it probably will save Fuller. Fuller's weak, but not broke. If a couple of Whitney's clients shift over, Fuller will probably pull through. There's a bit of irony, no?"

For the first time I saw the Judge in human form. An old man, who just lost his daughter and a step-son he never knew, surrounded by murder and suicide, and an incest scandal that he didn't even know about yet. I didn't have the heart to bring up the brother-sister thing, but I asked the obvious question instead: "What happens next?"

I think that the Judge began making up the answer on the spot. "You know, I was quite sick a year or so ago. My heart was bouncing all over the place. The pacemaker didn't seem to be doing the trick and I thought I was finished. But then I came around. I think it was Whizzie who really brought me back to life. She stayed with me through the whole thing, even offered to marry me. I know, she's pretty young for me, but she's been loyal. I'm thinking I'll quit this legal racket, retire, and see if Whizzie will still consider marrying me. There's enough money and there's always the Mansion. We can stay there, and maybe take some trips to the Islands." The Judge rambled on.

He was trying to dream up a future. I've wondered if what I did next was right. He had to find out one way or another. I reached into my breast pocket for the paper that Kathy had given me when we left the diner and handed it silently to the Judge. He read it slowly and the color drained from his face. At first I thought he would call the eager gun-toters who were waiting expectantly outside the door, but then any remnant of fight left him and he sagged into his chair. "They're married?"

"Yes."

"Sonny and Whizzie, married, for a year now?"

"They kept it secret to try not to hurt you too much," I lamely offered.

The Judge was stricken. The pacemaker had probably gone into overdrive. Whatever hopes and dreams he had been hanging on to, however unreal, were lying in a puddle under the massive desk. His eyes were hollow, and his $500 suit had become two sizes too large. I don't think he even remembered that I was there. "I'm going home now," he said flatly, as if I were his secretary. "Cancel all my appointments for the rest of today, and . . . tomorrow?" The sentence ended with a question mark.

I obliged. "It'll be taken care of, Judge. Don't worry."

He got up and walked out, leaving his briefcase and his coat. Went through the office and out, without a word to anyone. I gave some instructions to the secretary, and thanked the security guards as though I knew what I was doing. By the time I reached the courthouse steps he was gone. The taste of tragedy was in the air. Best to find Kathy.

29

THE POLICE HEADQUARTERS STOOD around the corner about a half block away from the courthouse. I walked around to the back of the station to what used to be a one-night-stand hotel that had been transformed into the police station annex. Here it was also difficult for civilians to get by the guards, but my past history with the department had left enough of an impression to allow me to enter unchallenged. I took the steps, two at a time, to the third floor.

JJ's front room was empty except for Kathy, whose back was toward me as she pored over a stack of Xerox copies. I came up behind her quietly, placed a forefinger just under her ear, and slid it slowly down the curve of her neck. I imagined myself skiing down a beautiful white slope ready to take off into the air just as I touched the brassiere strap. Kathy didn't move, waited a bit, and then said, "Good morning, Blue. What gets you up this early? It's barely noon." I knew I'd come for a reason, but the curve of her neck had obliterated it from my consciousness, so I just stood and looked stupid. She turned and smiled.

I remembered. "Let's talk. Got a minute?"

"Always," she answered. "JJ is not in—let's use the inner office." His office used to be a bedroom suite on the third floor of the old hotel and I wondered what scenarios had been played out on the spot where his work table now stood. Kathy settled easily into JJ's swivel chair as though it belonged to her. "What's up?" She broke my silence.

I gave Kathy a run-down: the Hernandez connection, the tail, the skinny on Whitney's schemes, his plan to merge and drop his losses onto the naïve Fuller, and the Judge waking up to the pressure and ruling against the merger, even though he realizes that his career and his dream are headed down the drain. Finally, I told her of his heart problems and then his fantasy of marrying and running off with Whizzie.

"I showed him the marriage certificate you dug up. I don't think I've ever seen a man crumble like he did as he read that paper."

Kathy suddenly sat up and leaned forward. "What did you say about the Judge's heart problems?"

"Just that. He's had a bad heart for years, but a year or so back he got to suffering from some pretty bad arrhythmia. Then it seemed to settle down. I think Whizzie's care during that time was pretty important to him."

"Blue!" Kathy looked directly at me. "Castor died from an overdose of fox glove, 'Dead Man's Bells.' That's digitalis."

"Yes?" I could see that Kathy was way ahead of me.

"Heart arrhythmia!" Kathy answered triumphantly. "Digitalis is prescribed in very small doses to calm the heart, slow it down. If given in larger doses it can cause the heart to jump all over the place. For a weak heart it could be fatal, and the fact that it shows up in an autopsy would not raise suspicion. And if someone gets a big dose of it, they can die pretty quickly. Unfortunately, it's a rather horrible death."

"How do you know this stuff?" I countered.

"When I found that marriage certificate I thought that I should follow up a bit. I took the info and did a bit of prowling around on Whizzie's background. Irene Wiseman. I'm not sure what happened to the family but she didn't seem to be in touch with them. She was a bright, sexy kid who was on her own and struggling just to stay afloat. No money, no family, no future. She was working in sales jobs mostly; the last one was over at Pharm-a-Lot Industries. That's in your neck of the woods, and you can be sure they manufacture digitalis."

"Yes it is." I thought for a moment. "Some nights the metaphysical shudders go to work on my brain, so I get sleeping pills at the Pharm-a-Lot retail store and she worked behind the counter a couple of years ago. I saw her there again, last week. Last Tuesday, picking up some pills."

Kathy's imagination was now taking off. Give her a few facts and she could write a novel. "I figure she met the Judge by chance somewhere," she continued. Then, inventing a bit, "How about she runs some errands for the retail side of Pharm-a-Lot and delivers his heart meds, his digitalis?"

"Took one look at the Mansion and went for it, moved in on the Judge," I said, agreeing. "She's not the type to worry about using her body, and the Judge is an obvious pushover," I added, mostly to show Kathy that I did have some expertise. "But what are you getting at?"

"Blue, throw a switch and put your mind on a different one-track." Kathy was talking quickly now. "Look, pharmaceuticals, he's taking digitalis to calm his heart. Then his heart starts to flutter. Who do you think is giving him the digitalis?

Judge gets sicker. Whizzie offers to marry him. She's figured out a way to bump him off by upping the digitalis dosage and no one will notice because his heart is already weak. Plans to marry him and get the Mansion and everything else after he dies. But somewhere along the way," Kathy was really wound up now, "she checks the Judge's copy of the will just to see what she is going to get, and suddenly she realizes that her quarry really doesn't own anything."

"Right, so she gives up on him," I followed her train of thought. "Nurses him back to health—no use giving him a heart attack for no reason. Then, following the dollar trail, she puts the make on Sonny. Even gets him to secretly marry her."

Kathy had more. "That's fine until Cass calls. On Wednesday he called Sonny, and he also called the Judge's office. But you told me the Judge said he'd never heard anything about Cass before the party."

"Of course, Whizzie took the call. She finds out that Cass is related and getting curious about some inheritance. She doesn't give the Judge the message." I was feeling smarter now.

Kathy kept on. "After the phone call, Whizzie checks the will again, discovers the meaning of the first-born line, and realizes that Cass is the rightful heir. Next thing you know, Cass dies . . . from an overdose of digitalis."

"An overdose of the heart medication," I repeated.

Kathy looked at me with a "good for you" expression that a mother might give her twelve-year-old for a B-plus on a math test. "She's the hostess at the reception, making sure everyone gets food and drink. She's already got a supply of the drug on hand, so she dumps a pile into Castor's punch. Her timing wasn't bad either. She's probably figured out that he's headed for the gatehouse, thinks maybe the poison will kick in when he's with Helen, and throw investigators off the track."

I remembered the punch. "It already tasted like kerosene. You could have dropped a horse turd in it and no one would have known." Then it dawned on me. "The Judge knows everything!" I almost shouted. "Once he sees the marriage license, he realizes that Whizzie, his dream, the only thing left of his future, is only after the money. It won't take him long to realize that when he was having heart problems, she was trying to bump him off, that she tried to kill him, but then shifted to Sonny when she found out that's where the money was."

We both moved at once. Down the stairs, out the back door, and into Kathy's coupe. I called JJ on the way to the Mansion.

30

I COULD SEE THAT the front door of the Mansion was open before Kathy braked to a halt on the gravel. We were out of the car, up the stairs, through the open door and into the living room in a dead run. The first thing that struck me was the open gun cabinet, and it was apparent that a couple of the pistols were missing. Wasn't it Checkhov who said that if you saw a gun in Act I, it would go off in Act III? And Hitchcock said that the most boring conversation would become spellbinding if the audience knew that there was a dead body in the closet. And who said never put a gun in the hands of a private eye unless he knows what to do with it? Actually that was me. I took the third pistol anyway.

Kathy was making a quick tour of the living room when a sharp snap ripped through the air, clearly a shot. She pointed in the direction of Sonny's room and we ran out to the terrace and around to the side door. The door was open and we found Sonny bent over a figure lying on the floor, a body lying face down and shaking. I called out something professional like "What the fuck?" and Sonny stood and turned towards me. He was holding a pistol and so was I. Jesus, right out of *High Noon*, with Gary Cooper nowhere in sight to save the day. Kathy ignored Sonny, and ran straight to the figure. If someone needed help, no gun was going to stop Kathy. She rolled the body over. Whizzie's chest was covered with blood and her eyes were staring straight through the ceiling to somewhere beyond. Sonny was shaking and the gun was angled halfway between me and the floor, and looked damn deadly. I pointed my pistol at his thigh and pulled the trigger, just in case it was loaded. It wasn't. The door to the garden was open and Sonny bolted through it. I took off after him, around the corner and back up the front steps. He went through the front door, slamming it behind him and the damn thing locked. I headed for the terrace. I was looking forward to breaking the glass on one of those French doors, but they were unlocked. The Judge's office was as good a goal as any. I ran through the living room and had my hand on the knob when the crack of a second shot shook the glass pane. The scene I found inside was not that different from the one I'd just left: Sonny standing gun in hand and the Judge sitting stone dead in his chair with his mouth open, an expression of disbelief permanently set on his face, his blood splattered over the framed law degrees hanging behind him. Sonny turned, looked at me. *High Noon* redux. The fact that my gun wasn't loaded didn't stop me from pointing it at Sonny and commanding "Drop the gun!" The third shot was unexpected. Sonny's gun had hit the floor and fired, and I felt a yellow jacket sting me in the calf. Sonny was shaking uncontrollably. He dropped into a chair, head in his hands. I could see he was no longer a threat, and I turned toward the Judge. He was welded to his chair like a bronze statue to justice seated in a courthouse lobby.

Shouts were coming from the living room. Kathy, JJ, Corbutt, and a couple of patrolmen burst into the room. It took about five seconds for the cops to cuff Sonny and drag the stunned figure out of the room. I looked at Kathy. She answered the unspoken question. "Whizzie's dead."

JJ was calling his forensic team on his cell. I looked down—damn yellow jacket got blood all over my pants. Kathy spotted the blood and let out a sympathetic "Ooh," knelt before me and pulled up the pant's cuff to display a bloody calf. She breathed a sigh of relief, and then said, "Looks like you'll still be riding your horse, Kid. Just a nick— we'll get that patched up right away." I wasn't going to get much sympathy from a scratch, but maybe if I limped a bit.

The room was a stage set—the last act of a tragedy. The Judge was a grotesque figure in his chair. He seemed to sit in control of the room. Two more police officers had entered, and were opening their cases, set to record crime-scene data: gathering fingerprints, DNA, and photos. For the moment they gave the presiding Judge a wide range. As I stared at the Judge, fascinated by the authority that he still wielded, I felt Kathy's hand slide across my ass. Without shifting my gaze, I reached down and caught her grip as her hand slid around my hip. She was stronger than I had remembered. I looked up and met Kathy's eyes across the room. She was looking at me and smiling curiously. I turned, then abruptly dropped Corbutt's hand. He gave me a knowing look and quickly left the room, turning a bit to allow his shoulders to pass through the narrow door. There was a dead man in the room with the presence of a sphinx. The wall behind was a combination of the Judge's brains and his awards. Kathy was next to him with the curious smile. Corbutt had left and I pondered how he would greet me tomorrow at the precinct. JJ busied himself with the police work, looking for every detail of the murder, and pretending to see nothing else.

He started talking. "So what do you think? Sonny figured Whizzie was after his money and blew up. He is a hot head. But he wouldn't shoot his father, the Judge, would he?"

"There were two guns gone from the cabinet," I added. "Maybe the Judge grabbed the other one to defend Whizzie, or . . . ?"

"He was just sitting in his chair," JJ continued. "Something's missing." That apparently was one of JJ's key phrases in solving a crime. The Judge's hands lay strangely in his lap, as if carelessly tossed there, and blood had begun to run from his open mouth. His legs pointed straight forward as though he was trying to push himself backwards. On the floor between the shined shoes I saw what was missing. The second gun. I pointed to it and JJ, in his best cop manner, took out a handkerchief and carefully picked it up. How come, in the age of Kleenex, detectives always have a handkerchief on hand, and what if they had a cold, wouldn't the mucous mess up the fingerprints and pollute the DNA, and what if . . . .

"It's been fired," JJ said. He had opened the chamber. "This pistol's been fired twice!"

Kathy, who apparently came up with her own handkerchief, was holding the gun that Sonny had been waving around. She carefully did the same, tilting the barrel forward to check the remaining bullets. "This one's only been fired once, and that's what hit Blue in the leg."

I was thankful that there hadn't been any bullets in my gun. Sonny may be an ass, but he doesn't deserve to get shot for trying to protect his wife.

"Fired twice," JJ repeated. "Once when the Judge shoots Whizzie, and once when he blows out his own brains. Two for two."

31

I WAS GLAD KATHY was driving. The evening was behind us, the sky was clear, the full moon was on the horizon, and a cold night was approaching. I was in no state to try to navigate any kind of vehicle down one side of a road, and the groove that Sonny's unintended bullet had carved in my leg was making itself known. Kathy had found a first-aid kit, smeared a bit of antiseptic cream on the furrow left by Sonny's bullet, and patched the hole with a band aid. Still it was beginning to throb.

We drove silently for a while, then Kathy began: "So Sonny never shot his gun. He came home, saw the cabinet was open, guessed the Judge had taken a pistol, and grabbed one for himself. They both seemed to have the foresight to load them," Kathy said, looking over at me.

"Or maybe they were already loaded, two of 'em, and not the third," I offered lamely.

Kathy continued. "Sonny follows him, finds him fighting or arguing or something with Whizzie. The Judge shoots Whizzie just as Sonny arrives. We turn up and Sonny runs after the Judge. I doubt he could kill his own father, even to save Whizzie. He went after him to warn him about us, or keep him from shooting himself. But he's too late. When he gets to the office, the Judge puts the barrel of his pistol in his mouth and pulls the trigger."

"Bloody Hell!" I offered to the plot, and then a bit more rationally, "Sonny's left with everything, and left with nothing. His twin sister committed suicide. Her lover, his half-brother, was poisoned by his wife. Now she's dead, shot by his father, who kills himself right in front of Sonny. Bloody Hell!"

"And Whitney Senior, what happens to him?"

"Even though he tried, he never actually did anything. He's too rich to serve time. These guys never get caught."

"He may headed for the poor house now," added Kathy.

"You're probably right. Unless he can find a rich estate to plunder, he may even have to fire Tweedledum and Tweedledee. Maybe he'll be able to get a job as an usher at *The Swan*."

"*The Swan*?"

"Fuller's going to fund the theatre and rename it *The Swan*."

"Leda and the Swan," Kathy said.

Another long silence. We drove up and stopped in front of Dung Hill Arms.

"Kathy. Could you love a fake?"

"Lawrence Olivier is a fake. An actor. Every time he says a line it's a ruse, a pretension, a lie . . . , and I love him.

"Life is a joke, only apparent to the comedian," I said.

"Life is a farce, only known to the clown," she countered.

"Life is a ruse, seen only by the magician."

"It takes a fake to tell a fake."

"You know, it's Monday night," I said.

"Yes it is." Kathy shivered. "First frost of the season tonight."

"Kathy, have you ever thought of just dropping everything and leaving, and becoming a hoba? Free as a bird?"

"Hoba?"

"I really don't want to go home alone tonight."

Kathy pushed a brown wisp of hair from over her eye, looked at me, and said nothing.

"Want to come in?" I asked.

"Yes," Kathy answered, but neither of us moved.

About the Author

This is a first novel by Michael Burke, best known as a sculptor and graphic artist. The son of philosopher Kenneth Burke, he has shown here a remarkable ability to connect contemporary life with ancient mythology. The result is sexy, thought-provoking, insightful, and a damned good read. Burke lives and works in New York City, and he is already well along on the next "Blue" Heron novel, another myth-based mystery with intrigue, lust, and more than one good laugh.

BOOKS FROM PLEASURE BOAT STUDIO: A LITERARY PRESS

(Note: Caravel Books is a new mystery imprint of Pleasure Boat Studio: A Literary Press. Caravel Books is the imprint for mysteries only. Aequitas Books is another imprint which includes non-fiction with philosophical and sociological themes. Empty Bowl Press is a Division of Pleasure Boat Studio.)

The Lord God Bird ~ Russell Hill ~ $15 ~ a caravel mystery

Island of the Naked Women ~ Inger Frimansson, trans. fm. Swedish by Laura Wideburg ~ $18 ~ a caravel mystery

Crossing the Water: The Hawaii-Alaska Trilogies ~ Irving Warner ~ fiction ~ $16

Among Friends ~ Mary Lou Sanelli ~ $15 ~ an aequitas book

Unnecessary Talking: The Montesano Stories ~ Mike O'Connor ~ $16

God Is a Tree, and Other Middle-Age Prayers ~ Esther Cohen ~ poems ~ $10

Home & Away: The Old Town Poems ~ Kevin Miller ~ $15

Old Tale Road ~ Andrew Schelling ~ $15 ~ an empty bowl book

Listening to the Rhino ~ Dr. Janet Dallett ~ $16 ~ an aequitas book

The Shadow in the Water ~ Inger Frimansson, trans. fm. Swedish by Laura Wideburg ~ $18 ~ a caravel mystery

The Woman Who Wrote "King Lear," And Other Stories ~ Louis Phillips ~ $16

Working the Woods, Working the Sea ~ Eds. Finn Wilcox and Jerry Gorsline ~ $22 ~ an empty bowl book

Weinstock Among the Dying ~ Michael Blumenthal ~ fiction ~ $18

The War Journal of Lila Ann Smith ~ Irving Warner ~ historical fiction ~ $18

Dream of the Dragon Pool: A Daoist Quest ~ Albert A. Dalia ~ fantasy ~ $18

Good Night, My Darling ~ Inger Frimansson, trans. fm. Swedish by Laura Wideburg ~ $16 ~ a caravel mystery

Falling Awake: An American Woman Gets a Grip on the Whole Changing World — One Essay at a Time ~ Mary Lou Sanelli ~ $15 ~ an aequitas book

Way Out There: Lyrical Essays ~ Michael Daley ~ $16 ~ an aequitas book

The Case of Emily V. ~ Keith Oatley ~ $18 ~ a caravel mystery

Monique ~ Luisa Coehlo, trans. fm. Portuguese by Maria do Carmo de Vasconcelos and Dolores DeLuise ~ fiction ~ $14

The Blossoms Are Ghosts at the Wedding ~ Tom Jay ~ essays & poems ~ $15 ~ an empty bowl book

Against Romance ~ Michael Blumenthal ~ poetry ~ $14

Speak to the Mountain: The Tommie Waites Story ~ Dr. Bessie Blake ~ 278 pages ~ biography ~ $18 / $26 ~ an aequitas book

Artrage ~ Everett Aison ~ fiction ~ $15

Days We Would Rather Know ~ Michael Blumenthal ~ poetry ~ $14

Puget Sound: 15 Stories ~ C. C. Long ~ fiction ~ $14

Homicide My Own ~ Anne Argula ~ fiction (mystery) ~ $16

Craving Water ~ Mary Lou Sanelli ~ poetry ~ $15

When the Tiger Weeps ~ Mike O'Connor ~ poetry and prose ~ 15

Wagner, Descending: The Wrath of the Salmon Queen ~ Irving Warner ~ fiction ~ $16

Concentricity ~ Sheila E. Murphy ~ poetry ~ $13.95

Schilling, from a study in lost time ~ Terrell Guillory ~ fiction ~ $17

Rumours: A Memoir of a British POW in WWII ~ Chas Mayhead ~ nonfiction ~ $16

The Immigrant's Table ~ Mary Lou Sanelli ~ poetry and recipes ~ $14

The Enduring Vision of Norman Mailer ~ Dr. Barry H. Leeds ~ criticism ~ $18

Women in the Garden ~ Mary Lou Sanelli ~ poetry ~ $14

Pronoun Music ~ Richard Cohen ~ short stories ~ $16

If You Were With Me Everything Would Be All Right ~ Ken Harvey ~ short stories ~ $16

The 8th Day of the Week ~ Al Kessler ~ fiction ~ $16

Another Life, and Other Stories ~ Edwin Weihe short stories ~ $16

Saying the Necessary ~ Edward Harkness ~ poetry ~ $14

Nature Lovers ~ Charles Potts ~ poetry ~ $10

In Memory of Hawks, & Other Stories from Alaska ~ Irving Warner ~ fiction ~ $15

The Politics of My Heart ~ William Slaughter ~ poetry ~ $13

The Rape Poems ~ Frances Driscoll ~ poetry ~ $13

When History Enters the House: Essays from Central Europe ~ Michael Blumenthal ~ nonfiction ~ $15

Setting Out: The Education of Lili ~ Tung Nien ~ trans. fm Chinese by Mike O'Connor ~ fiction ~ $15

OUR CHAPBOOK SERIES:

No. 1: *The Handful of Seeds: Three and a Half Essays* ~ Andrew Schelling ~ $7 ~ nonfiction

No. 2: *Original Sin* ~ Michael Daley ~ $8 ~ poetry

No. 3: *Too Small to Hold You* ~ Kate Reavey ~ $8 ~ poetry

No. 4: *The Light on Our Faces: A Therapy Dialogue* ~ Lee Miriam Whitman-Raymond ~ $8 ~ poetry

No. 5: *Eye* ~ William Bridges ~ $8 ~ poetry

No. 6: *Selected New Poems of Rainer Maria Rilke* ~ trans. fm German by Alice Derry ~ $10 ~ poetry

No. 7: *Through High Still Air: A Season at Sourdough Mountain* ~ Tim McNulty ~ $9 ~ poetry, prose

No. 8: *Sight Progress* ~ Zhang Er, trans. fm Chinese by Rachel Levitsky ~ $9 ~ prosepoems

No. 9: *The Perfect Hour* ~ Blas Falconer ~ $9 ~ poetry

No. 10: *Fervor* ~ Zaedryn Meade ~ $10 ~ poetry

No. 11: *Some Ducks* ~ Tim McNulty ~ $10 ~ poetry

No. 12: *Late August* ~ Barbara Brackney ~ $10 ~ poetry

No. 13: *The Right to Live Poetically* ~ Emily Haines ~ $10 ~ poetry

FROM OTHER PUBLISHERS (in limited editions):

Desire ~ Jody Aliesan ~ $14 ~ poetry (an empty bowl book)

Deams of the Hand ~ Susan Goldwitz ~ $14 ~ poetry (an empty bowl book)

Lineage ~ Mary Lou Sanelli ~ $14 ~ poetry (an empty bowl book)

The Basin: Poems from a Chinese Province ~ Mike O'Connor ~ $10 / $20 ~ poetry (paper/ hardbound) (an empty bowl book)

The Straits ~ Michael Daley ~ $10 ~ poetry (an empty bowl book)

In Our Hearts and Minds: The Northwest and Central America ~ Ed. Michael Daley ~ $12 ~ poetry and prose (an empty bowl book)

The Rainshadow ~ Mike O'Connor ~ $16 ~ poetry (an empty bowl book)

Untold Stories ~ William Slaughter ~ $10 / $20 ~ poetry (paper / hardbound) (an empty bowl book)

In Blue Mountain Dusk ~ Tim McNulty ~ $12.95 ~ poetry (a Broken Moon book)

China Basin ~ Clemens Starck ~ $13.95 ~ poetry (a Story Line Press book)

Journeyman's Wages ~ Clemens Starck ~ $10.95 ~ poetry (a Story Line Press book)

Orders: Pleasure Boat Studio books are available by order from your bookstore, directly from PBS, or through the following:

SPD (Small Press Distribution)
Tel. 800-869-7553, Fax 510-524-0852
Partners/West
Tel. 425-227-8486, Fax 425-204-2448
Baker & Taylor
Tel. 800-775-1100, Fax 800-775-7480
Ingram
Tel. 615-793-5000, Fax 615-287-5429
Amazon.com or **Barnesandnoble.com**

Pleasure Boat Studio: A Literary Press
201 West 89th Street
New York, NY 10024
Tel / Fax: 888-810-5308
www.pleasureboatstudio.com /
pleasboat@nyc.rr.com